Sarah's Garden

Sarah's Garden

Lisa Smelter

gatekeeper press™
Columbus, Ohio

Sarah's Garden
Published by Gatekeeper Press
2167 Stringtown Rd, Suite 109
Columbus, OH 43123-2989
www.GatekeeperPress.com

The editorial work for this book is entirely the product of the author. Gatekeeper Press did not participate in and is not responsible for any aspect of this element.

Copyright for the images: iStockphoto.com/fotostorm (woman), Akabei (garden).

Library of Congress Control Number: 2021949821

ISBN (hardcover): 9781662922022
ISBN (paperback): 9781662921223
eISBN: 9781662920943

CHAPTER
ONE

No one looking at the exterior of the big ugly Victorian house would guess at the charm of the top floor suite. The other three suites in the building housed a young married couple--just setting up house, a group of three young college women, and the landlady. In the top suite lived a young woman, all by herself, now that her mother had passed away. The room was large, with a sloped roof. It was divided into a few separate small rooms.

Sarah, a happy girl by nature, was sitting in one of the overstuffed armchairs crying softly. Mrs. Brewster's funeral had been just yesterday, and Sarah was feeling her loss quite overwhelmingly. Sarah looked around the pretty and well-furnished room and felt comforted. As she sat there, she remembered her mom and dad. Her dad had been a sweetie. He had been gone a long time. Her mom had been a sweet and gentle woman. She had had a happy, but much too short, marriage to her dear husband. Together, they had given Sarah such a wonderful start in life. She was every bit her father's and mother's daughter.

Daniel Brewster had been a gentle, unpretentious man. He had been an orphan since the age of fifteen when his parents had died in a fire. He lived with his aunt and uncle until he graduated from high school. With the untimely death of his aunt and uncle in a car crash when he was twenty, he was totally alone in the world. After spending a few years in the Army, he looked around for other work. He took on odd jobs, finally working at a landscaping business. He found that he loved working in the soil, nurturing plants and flowers. It did not pay him much money, but it made his soul happy. While he was working there, he met his young wife. She had come into the nursery for some flowers. Dan had taken one look at her and knew that she was the one woman in the world for him. She was also a gentle soul, and they married as soon as they could scrape together enough money to do so.

They had been so happy when Sarah was born. She was a pretty little thing, with a very sunny outlook on life. They bought a small house on the edge of town. There was room in the backyard for a garden and a swing set, not much else. Sarah's earliest memories were of helping her father plant seedlings and tending the plants. She always had flowers planted in Styrofoam cups and milk cartons on the windowsill in her room. Her grandmother's cobalt blue glass vase, which was her father's only remaining childhood treasure, always had flowers in it. Sarah remembered her father saying, "Flowers are God's way of painting a beautiful palette on the world." Sarah and her parents did not have much in the way of material goods, but they had a happy and meaningful life together.

Sarah smiled when she remembered her father coming home from work, pleased about something that had happened that day. He would waltz her mother around the kitchen, saying, "Tilly, I have a good life. I have a beautiful wife, a delightful daughter, and enough money to buy what I really need. What could be better than that?" Her mom would laugh softly, and they would dance for a few minutes. After a few minutes of dancing with her mom, Daddy always grabbed Sarah, and the three of them would dance around and around the kitchen. They would end up laughing and, out of breath, would sit down at the kitchen table.

Sarah remembered how they would talk about any purchase they wanted to make. There was never enough money to just go out and buy it; they had to plan out the purchase.

Her father used to say, "It's better to save for something really special than to buy just any old thing. It's quality that counts, not quantity." They used to save any extra money that was left over at the end of the week in a plastic flower-imprinted container that had come from her father's work. He was proud of that container. It was his recommendation to his boss to use the attractive containers to sell their peat and other landscape supplies. Homemakers could reuse the pretty container for other things once it was empty of its original contents. That had earned him a raise and the respect of his boss.

Her father had also recommended that they sell flower sticker books for the children. The stickers would show off all of the varieties of flowers that the company sold. Over the years, Sarah had gotten many of these sticker books. Her father always bought the newest sticker book when it came out. She would find them, wrapped in pretty paper next to her breakfast bowl in the mornings. By the time she was six years old, Sarah could name all the flowers, including their Latin names, that were sold at her father's work.

Sarah's father had found delight in his little daughter. Sarah was a sweet little chatterbox. Daniel was a man of few words, as was his gentle wife, and they always marveled at their extreme good fortune at having such a happy little girl. His pet name for her was Sunshine.

He would say, "Sarah Sunshine, what's new with you?" or "Sunshine, tell me something happy that happened to you today." This made Sarah always look for the happy things in life. Sarah and her father had their love of flowers and all growing things in common. They used to sit for hours looking at pictures of flowers and other plants, looking up their Latin names and how to grow them.

Sarah also loved one-on-one time with her mother. Tilly was a lovely young woman. She loved her husband and her dear little daughter. She also loved the Lord. She taught Sarah Bible stories and talked about how to try to be a good servant to God and to others. For all of Tilly's shy and gentle ways, she had many friends. This was because she was such a good listener. She said that some people just needed to talk and be heard. They always felt better after they talked their way through some issue or problem. Sometimes they just had something really sweet or exciting that they wanted to share with someone. Sarah learned at an early age how to listen to people. She was more outgoing than either one of her parents, but she still had a lot of shyness inside herself, as well.

When their beloved Bernese Mountain Dog came into their lives, it completed their family. Sarah could still remember going to the Animal Humane Society and seeing Wolfie for the first time. It was love at first sight for both Sarah and the dog. She knew at that moment that he must become part of their family. Her father had told Sarah that it would be her responsibility to care for him. She had taken that job lovingly. He slept in her room and went everywhere with her. It had been a struggle to teach Wolfie not to dig up Dan's plants in the backyard, but he eventually understood that there was to be no digging in his backyard--only the small designated spot that he was given. Sarah thought of Wolfie as her younger brother.

They had several happy years together until he was killed, along with her father, in a tragic car accident a month after Sarah's ninth birthday. Life changed so much that day. Sarah and her mom had to pull themselves together and go on with life, even though they were shattered by their loss.

The day had to be gotten through. With the funeral and guests, yesterday had been filled with a hundred and one chores. Now, today, reality intervened. Sarah had to start making some plans. She opened the "Help Wanted" pages of the local newspaper and began to search for employment. Now that she no longer had to care for her mother, she needed to find a job that would not only provide her needed funds but also fill the hours of loneliness she was preparing herself to face. Her office skills were a little rusty since she had not worked outside her home for nearly two years. She would have to brush up on her skills before she took a new job. Their old computer sat neglected and dusty in the back closet. Sarah searched thoroughly, but she could not find anything suitable for herself.

Sarah's best friend, Susan, called. "Sarah, do you want some company tonight? I thought that I might come over, and we could make supper and talk. What do you think?" Sarah was grateful for this respite from her own thoughts.

"Yes, please, Susan. I don't want to be alone with my thoughts this evening. I would love to have company. Why don't you stay over and go to work from here, tomorrow? I have some great lasagna left over from yesterday."

Susan agreed and said she would be there in an hour or so. Sarah went into the kitchen to see what other goodies she had in the fridge. After the funeral yesterday, they had a catered meal from her mother's favorite pasta restaurant. It had been her mother's final wish that they celebrate her life with a good meal from there.

All of their friends had come, and they had talked for hours about Tilly. They had all gone to the cemetery first, to see Tilly buried next to her beloved husband.

Because it was a cold and snowy day, no one stayed very long in the cemetery. Sarah had stayed longer, after everyone else had gone, talking to her parents. It was a habit that her mom had started. When Daniel died, Sarah's mom had started taking her to visit her father's grave after church every Sunday. They told him everything that was going on in their lives--their triumphs and their trials. This little habit kept Daniel close to them in all the years of his absence. Now Sarah would have both of her parents to visit on Sundays.

Susan came over, her dark hair covered with snowflakes. She dumped her overnight bag in Sarah's bedroom and came in to give Sarah a big hug. "Brrr! It's cold out there! How are you holding up? Today was a pretty dismal day for you, wasn't it?"

Sarah nodded and said, "I was so busy yesterday that I didn't have time to think. Now, today, that's all I have been doing. Thank you, Susan, for being there for me yesterday. It was the saddest day of my life."

Susan hugged her and said, "Sarah, I love you. I loved your mom, too. Of course, I would be there for you. I was happy to see so many of your mom's friends, too. It was a beautiful service. The flowers in the church were so lovely. What did you do with all of them?"

Sarah smiled a little sadly and said, "I left most of them in the church. They looked so nice. I put some of them on Mom's grave. Of course, they won't last long with all the cold and snow, but I think my mom would have liked to have them on her grave. I put a few on Daddy's grave, too."

Susan took Sarah's arm, and they went into the small kitchen. She saw the beautiful flower arrangement in the blue vase. "Where did you get these beautiful flowers?" she asked.

Sarah bent to smell them and smiled, "Mrs. Johnson, my landlady, brought them over. Aren't they gorgeous? Mom would have loved them," she said, with a catch in her voice.

Susan hugged her again and said, "Just you cry if you want, love. You will feel better afterwards."

Sarah said, "Thanks, but I have already cried so much that I don't think that I have much left in me." They went through the fridge and made themselves a delicious supper. After supper, they sat in the living room, talking and reminiscing. At some point, Sarah said, "I'll have to get a job. Mom's life insurance barely covered the funeral costs. I only have enough money left for a few months."

Susan nodded, looking concerned, and asked, "What kind of work do you want to get?"

Sarah said, "Well, I was a secretary before I gave up my job to nurse Mom. Of course, that was two years ago. I think that would be the best fit for me. I know the work and like it. I wonder if there have been any new developments in office technology since I left."

Susan smiled wryly and said, "Yes--those things seem to change daily, don't they? Maybe you should take a refresher course at the college."

Together the two friends searched the internet for suitable computer refresher courses nearby. They found one that looked good, and it was offering a comprehensive course that would be starting in two weeks.

Sarah learned an incredible amount of new material in her computer course. There were new applications and platforms that she had not worked with before but were all the rage in the business world. She also brushed up on her shorthand and telephone skills.

The day after Sarah finished the course, Michael, her instructor, asked her out for supper. She thought that he was nice, and they had so much in common. They went to Sarah's favorite restaurant.

Michael couldn't take his eyes off her. He thought that she was so sweet and pretty. Her light brown hair was long and very shiny, hanging down her back to her waist. Her eyes were a lovely soft green, and she had a wholesome clear complexion. She had a natural and gentle kind of beauty. Sarah smiled a lot, showing her small white teeth. She was always dressed in such feminine clothes--long swirly skirts and pretty tops. Her earrings were long and dangling and matched her skirt. Besides all that, she had a delicious sense of humor, finding humorous things to talk about, but never at anyone's expense. That's what he liked the best about her. She had a kind soul, always thinking about other people before herself. They had a very nice evening, and she agreed to go out with him again.

Sarah saw quite a lot of Michael for a few weeks. He called her every few days. He wanted to be with her every possible moment. She liked him but was not interested in getting seriously involved with him. She thought of him as a friend. She eventually had to tell him that she wouldn't go out with him anymore. He was becoming too intense for her comfort. He angrily took her home and drove away. She felt bad that she had just lost a friend.

Now that she had taken the refresher course, Sarah felt able to look for a job again. She diligently searched the "Help Wanted" ads every day without much luck. After a few weeks of looking, she finally found what she thought would be the perfect job. It was located only eight miles from her home and was in a large business center near some shops and a little park. Sarah sent in her online application to interview for the job at Thompson Engineering. She received a phone call requesting her to come in for an interview at 2:00 pm the next day. She was to be prepared to show her phone and computer skills during the interview. Sarah nervously accepted the request.

Sarah had heard of Thompson Engineering and knew that the owner was a quiet and professional man. Someone like that might want his employees to be dressed conservatively and professionally. She took stock of her clothing. Most of her clothes were soft, colorful, and feminine--hardly suitable for work in a professional office. However, she remembered that her mother had several black and navy blue skirts. Since she and her mom had been close to the same size, Sarah decided to search through her closet. She was happy that she had not yet done anything about giving away her mother's clothing and other personal effects. Since most of their lives they had lived in small apartments and had limited space, Sarah and her mother had never hung onto things that they no longer needed. They were definitely not what you would call packrats. The Goodwill in town had benefited often from their charitable giving.

Sarah found two nice black skirts, an elegant pleated navy blue skirt, and several silky white blouses that could go with any of the three skirts. The navy blue skirt fit her perfectly, as did a long sleeved white silk blouse that had a nice bow tie at the neck. With her dark nylons and blue pumps, Sarah felt that she looked as professional as she could get. Now, what to do with her long hair? She decided to put it into a loose ponytail, tied with a blue ribbon. She never could get her hair to stay in a bun on top of her head. Her hair was so silky and fine that it came loose too quickly. A ponytail was neat, and it would not take a long time to fix in the mornings.

Sarah arrived for her interview fifteen minutes early. She walked up to the woman behind the desk and said brightly, "Hello. My name is Sarah Brewster, and I have a 2:00 pm meeting with Mr. Thompson."

The secretary smiled in a friendly way at Sarah and said, "Well, dear, why don't you go on over to those comfortable chairs and wait? You can look at those magazines while you are waiting. I will tell Mr. Thompson that you are here after the current applicant has finished interviewing with him."

Sarah nodded and went to sit down in the waiting room. While she waited, Sarah looked around her. The walls were painted a pale gray, the thick plush carpet was a darker gray, and the comfortable armchairs were navy blue. There were whispers of pale peach color splashed around in the wall hangings and in the chair cushions.

The decor was very tasteful and professional, as well as providing a calming effect on the people waiting in the room. Sarah, being a devotee of color themes, approved of the whole effect.

Sarah was called into Mr. Thompson's office at exactly 2:00 pm. Sitting behind the big desk was a very attractive man. Sarah took in his dark brown wavy hair, already silvered at his temples. His eyes were a bright blue, and he had a firm mouth and an autocratic nose. His face was tanned as if he had recently returned from a vacation in the sun. He was impeccably dressed in a dark gray suit, white silk shirt, and an Italian silk tie in a dark blue.

She sat in the chair that the man indicated. Her hands in her lap, she looked directly at him and waited for him to speak.

He stood up, reached his hand over the desk to shake her hand, and said, "Good afternoon Miss Brewster. I am Paul Thompson, owner of Thompson Engineering. Thank you for coming." His voice was deep and pleasant to listen to. He explained that he would like her to use the script that he gave her to answer some practice calls. She had a soft and very pleasant voice and got through the practice phone calls with no trouble. Mr. Thompson then asked her to use the computer that was sitting on a nearby small table to get into some applications and type up the data that was also on the stack of papers that he gave her. Again, these proved to be well within her skill set. When she had completed these tasks, he smiled and asked her to sit down.

"Now tell me about your two most recent jobs," he invited. She discussed her jobs, and the responsibilities specific to each one. She stated that she had enjoyed her previous jobs and had only left her last one to take care of her mother, who had recently passed away. She now wanted to restart her career.

Paul looked at her and gently said, "I am so sorry to hear about your mother. How long had you been her caregiver?" Sarah looked down at her hands in her lap, her eyes brimming with tears.

She softly said, "I left my job a little over two years ago when we found out that her illness was terminal. I wanted to spend as much time with her as I could. Her doctor said that she lived six months longer than he expected her to live, just because she was happy. That made me feel very happy, too. I have never regretted the time that I spent caring for her." He handed her a Kleenex and stood up to look out of the window. This gave Sarah a minute to pull herself together and wipe her eyes. She waited quietly for him to continue. He turned back around and saw that she was composed again.

He said, "My wonderful secretary of many years had to leave unexpectedly to take care of her ailing brother. She does not expect to return. I have been having to get by with a temporary secretary from an agency. I am looking for someone to fill Mrs. Graham's very commendable shoes. I would like my new secretary to start on Monday, if possible. My temporary secretary needs to have some time off to take care of personal business, and I don't want to get yet another temporary secretary. Should I decide to offer you the job, could you be ready to start on Monday?" Sarah stated that she would be able to do that.

Mr. Thompson stated that he had several other applicants to interview before he could make a decision. Someone from his office would let her know by Friday evening if she got the job.

Sarah smiled and said, "Thank you for interviewing me. I should be at home most of the time this week. If I have to go out, I'll be sure to check my messages. Goodbye, Mr. Thompson." She shook hands with him and walked out into the waiting room. She smiled at the two other women in the waiting room. One woman smiled back. The other one just looked nervous.

Sarah said gently, "Good luck to you both. He seems to be a very nice employer." She quietly left the room to go to her car.

As she drove home, Sarah thought about the interview. She had liked Mr. Thompson. He had shown compassion when she talked about her mom's death. He had given her time to compose herself, too. She would enjoy working for such a nice person. The salary that he offered was much better than she had received at her last job. If she could get this job and hang on to it for at least a few years, she would be able to save some money, again. Her savings had been almost wiped out, paying for extras that she had wanted her mom to have. Her mother's inheritance from her parents had barely covered the cost of the rent. Sarah's jobs had provided them with the money for food, clothes, and their entertainment. She had never wanted to move away from her mother. They got along so well together. Not including Susan, Sarah's mom had been her best friend. They had a comfortable and happy life until her mother became ill.

During the interview, Mr. Thompson had stated that he liked his employees to wear black, dark gray, or navy blue pants, skirts, or dresses. Accents of white were allowed. He preferred that his front office staff maintain a professional appearance because they were the first people that prospective clients would see. Sarah was very glad that she had dressed conservatively for the interview. If she got the job, she would have to invest in a few more professional outfits.

Paul Thompson finished his interviewing for the day. Only one candidate stuck out in his mind, and that was Sarah Brewster. Several of the applicants seemed so timid and were not quite proficient either speaking on the telephone or typing up the data that he gave them to do. Sarah had been quietly confident on both her telephone and computer tests. Paul went out to talk with his temporary secretary.

"Were any of the applicants here early today? Also, did you get a good feeling about anyone?" he asked her.

"Well, Mr. Thompson, that nice young girl, Sarah Brewster, was fifteen minutes early. She was ever so pleasant with the other applicants, too," she told him. He nodded. He had gained the same impression of Sarah, as well. Sarah had been professionally dressed, with no outlandish jewelry. He still couldn't believe that one of the applicants had worn a bright red pantsuit, along with large red hoop earrings and an annoying amount of jingling gold bracelets. He shook his head as he remembered her. Sarah had a pleasant voice, had done the practice scripts well, and obviously knew her way around a computer. He thought that Sarah Brewster would work very well. He decided to make the call to invite her to work for him.

Sarah was just about to make herself some supper when the phone rang on Friday evening. She picked up the phone and said hello in her pretty voice.

There was a silence on the other end for just a moment and then, "Hello, Miss Brewster. This is Paul Thompson. I am calling you to invite you to join our company."

Sarah happily said, "Thank you, Mr. Thompson. I would be happy to accept the position." Paul told her what time he would expect to see her on Monday and where she should park her car. He hung up after thanking her for agreeing to join his company. As he set the receiver down, he thought about her pleasant voice. It had been soft and sweet and had surprised him so much that he had not been able to speak for just a moment. He shook his head and went home, forgetting all about the office and the trials he had had that day. He just wanted to get home to his two dogs. He hoped that Mrs. Kennedy, his housekeeper, had left him something tasty for supper.

Sarah hung up the phone and danced her way around the room, just like her dad had always done when he was happy. She had gotten the job! She called Susan after she stopped dancing. "Susan, I got that job that I talked to you about!" Sarah said happily.

"Oh, that's wonderful, Sarah. Tell me about it. No, wait--let me come over, and I will bring something to celebrate your good fortune. See you in thirty minutes," Susan said, with a smile in her voice.

Susan came in like a whirlwind, laughing and talking a mile a minute. "Nothing but champagne would do to celebrate your new job, my dear," Susan said, laughing.

"Oh Susan, you didn't have to bring champagne! It's too expensive. We could have celebrated with something cheaper," Sarah stated.

"No, we definitely need champagne for this celebration. Besides, this is a small bottle, which didn't cost too much. This is the beginning of a brand new life for you. I just know that you will be great at this new job. Now tell me everything while I open this champagne," Susan instructed.

Sarah smiled and said, "Oh Susan, it's a dream job. My new boss is very handsome and seems so kind. We talked a little bit about my mom, and I started to tear up. He just smiled nicely at me, gave me a tissue, and went to stare out the window until I pulled myself back together."

Susan raised her eyebrows and asked, "How cute, and how old is he?"

Sarah laughed a little and said, "He's got dark wavy hair with a bit of gray at the temples. He looks to be about thirty-five years old, I think. He's probably married or something, but he just seemed very nice and kind. He was tanned and wore a very nice suit and elegant tie."

Susan asked, "Any more openings at that place? He sounds a lot better than my boss."

"Silly, you love your job, Susan. You have been there for five years. I think your boss would go crazy if you ever left," Sarah said with her eyebrows raised.

Susan smirked, "Yes, he really does need me, and he respects me. That place would fall apart without me," Susan said, proudly.

"I know," said Sarah, "It would have to be an exceptional job to make you leave that job. They wouldn't know what to do without you."

The two friends drank up the champagne and giggled and talked long into the evening about life in general. Sarah told Susan about Michael and their quarrel. Susan agreed that Sarah had to let him go. They talked about Susan's latest beau, as well. He was also becoming way too serious for Susan's peace of mind. She liked him well enough, but certain things about him got on her nerves. She was going to have to tell him that she wanted her space, as well.

They wondered if they would ever find the right man. He would have to be a man in a million to gain their love. This was a topic that the two friends had discussed quite often over the last five years. Sarah's mom used to tell them that somewhere out there, in the big wide world, was the man they would fall in love with, and love until the end of time. She had been so sure of that, that Sarah and Susan had been comforted. Susan kept trying to find Mr. Right, but Sarah never looked for him. She was not in a hurry. If there was a man out there for her, she felt in her heart that they would meet, sooner or later. In the meantime, she was content to just date her male friends in a very casual way. She was content with her life the way it was.

Susan agreed to come over on Saturday morning to help Sarah go through all of her mother's clothes and personal effects. But first, they planned to go shopping to augment Sarah's wardrobe for her new job.

CHAPTER

TWO

The next day at the mall, the two friends ran into another of Sarah's friends. Her name was Clara Burke, and she was a long-time friend of Sarah and Mrs. Brewster. Susan had met her on a number of occasions while she was hanging out with Sarah. Clara was carrying a very small Jack Russell puppy. Clara and Sarah hugged each other, with Susan looking on and smiling. They decided to chat with Clara in the Food Court before they started their shopping. Clara held firmly onto her little pup while they drank their cold beverages.

Sarah was curious, and so she asked Clara, "Tell me about this new member of your family, Clara. He certainly is different from King." King had been Clara's old Alaskan husky, who had died about five years previously.

Clara grinned and told them how she had acquired Rip. "Well, you know that I always have my daughter, Dana, her husband, and her two little ones over for Christmas, right? This year they came over on Christmas Eve with this little guy. They wanted me to have a new dog. He would be company for me, especially now that King and Bob are gone."

Clara looked very sad for a moment. Sarah reached out and grabbed Clara's hand and held on to it. Sarah nodded and waited for Clara to continue. "As soon as they got there, my grandson, Bobby, put the puppy down. This little guy immediately scuttled under the Christmas tree and started to rip into one of the presents that I had so painstakingly wrapped up for Christa. I guess it had a scent to it because it was one of those gift boxes of makeup, lip gloss, and perfume that little girls love. Luckily, he didn't harm the gift itself, only the wrapping paper. Before I could pick him up, he started to rip into another gift. Bobby caught him before he could destroy any other gifts. We had to hold onto him while the kids opened all of the gifts. When the gifts were all opened, I decided that he could play around in the used wrapping paper that we had put in a big pile. You should have seen him. He went crazy in that pile of paper. He turned around and around, sniffing it and tearing it up. He got himself so tuckered out that he finally lay down in the pile and went to sleep. Bobby said that they had wanted me to call him Max, but now he thought that the puppy's name should be Rip. Ron, Dana, and I laughed our heads off when Bobby said that. His name has been Rip ever since. Funnily enough, he doesn't bother anything else in the house, except for the toilet paper in the bathroom. I have to keep the door closed. The first time he ripped into it, there was a whole roll unraveled and ripped on the floor. What a mess that was." Clara chuckled and gave Rip a big kiss on the top of his head. "I have to keep him on a leash, otherwise I just know he would get himself into trouble whenever we go anywhere. Anyway, he keeps me young."

Sarah and Susan laughed at Clara's great story. Sarah asked to hold Rip because she loved all dogs. She caressed his silky ears and gently scratched the top of his small head. "Clara, I would be glad to puppysit for him if you ever needed me to do that. Remember how Mom and I used to dogsit for King? Susan, you even helped me dogsit for King a few times." They all smiled, remembering with fond memories, the sweet and gentle giant. King had been a very good friend to Clara and Bob. After Bob had died unexpectedly, Clara had really needed King's affectionate and undemanding company. Whenever she went to visit her son, Dylan, who lived a few hundred miles away, Sarah had stayed at Clara's house with King.

Clara smiled and said, "Sarah, you are such a good girl. I will probably take you up on that. I am planning to visit Dylan and his family in a few months. There is also my niece's wedding in July. I'll give you a call, okay?"

Sarah nodded and said, "Anytime, Clara. I've got to get to know this little guy better." Clara had to get going, so she picked up Rip and waved goodbye to the two girls.

Susan and Sarah spent the next few hours looking for clothes that would work well for Sarah's new job. Susan was a bit of a clothes horse and had worked in a business office for the last five years. She kept her eyes on what was new and fashionable for the working woman. She convinced Sarah to buy some very stylish, but professional, new clothes. Sarah had not planned to spend quite that much on her new clothes, but she felt better when she thought about her new salary. She wouldn't have to buy any new clothes for quite a long time. Quality vs quantity, her parents had always told her.

After supper, they went through all of Tilly's clothes, jewelry, and personal possessions. They laughed and cried, talking about Tilly and how wonderful she was. Susan had loved Tilly almost as much as her own mother. Tilly had made Susan feel welcome in their home for more than fifteen years. Sarah gave Susan a few pieces of Tilly's jewelry that she had always liked. Tilly had loved Susan and had thanked her many times for being such a loving and caring friend to her little Sarah. Sarah really needed Susan's loving friendship that night. It was heart-wrenching going through Tilly's things. Sarah had loved her mother so much. She had put off going through Tilly's things until Susan could be there with her.

They were always there for each other. Sarah spent any number of days at her friend's house after Susan eventually broke up with any of her boyfriends. Susan fell in and out of love regularly, but her relationships never seemed to last very long. Sarah thought that maybe that was because of Susan's parents' difficult divorce when she had been a young teenager. Whatever the reason, Susan moved on to new relationships quite frequently. In this way, the two friends were completely different. Sarah had never been in love before. She liked a good many of her young male friends, but none of them had ever touched her heart. So, at the ripe old age of twenty-five, Sarah was heart-whole.

Sarah found her mom's simple but beautiful wedding dress and veil while they were going through Tilly's closet. Because Sarah and Tilly were fairly close in shape and size, Sarah decided to try on the dress.

She said, "Susan, please help me put on this dress. I want to see how I look in Mom's wedding dress. Who knows if I will ever get married?" Susan helped Sarah into the dress and veil. It was like looking at Tilly in the mirror. They looked at Tilly and Daniel's wedding photo, which had the place of honor on Tilly's bedside table. It was uncanny how much Sarah looked like her mother, especially in the wedding dress.

"Oh, I need to put on Mom's wedding ring, too," declared Sarah. It was a bit snug on Sarah's finger. The two friends waltzed around the apartment, laughing and pretending that they were married ladies. Because they needed to keep working to get through all of Tilly's things, Sarah reluctantly took off the wedding dress and veil. She tried to take off Tilly's wedding ring, but it wouldn't come off.

"Help me, Susan," demanded Sarah, in a panic. "I can't get Mom's ring off my finger."

Susan said, "Put some dish soap on your finger. That should make your hand so slippery that the ring will come off." Susan ran to get the soap. They liberally soaped Sarah's hand. Sarah tugged for a few minutes until the ring finally came off.

"Whew, that was close! What if it wouldn't have come off?" asked Sarah, with a relieved voice.

"Well, if you ever want to wear it, you can always get it resized," said Susan, in a practical voice.

"I think that I will just keep it in its little velvet box inside my dresser drawer. I don't think that I will want to wear it. I just want to keep it to remind me of Mom," said Sarah.

They put the items that Sarah decided to keep back into Tilly's closet and closed the door. All of the rest they put into large clean garbage bags to take to Goodwill next week. Susan had taken a few things that Sarah wanted her to have.

Before she left, she helped Sarah get her things ready for her first day of work on Monday. They decided which of Sarah's small treasures she should take to work with her. They didn't gather many things together because Sarah was unsure that her new boss would let her put any of them on her desk.

Sarah decided to take her mug, a small picture of Tilly, and her favorite matching notebook and pen to work with her on Monday. Sarah's favorite ceramic coffee mug was a beautifully shaped one covered in raised and colorful summer flowers. On the underside of the mug was a small defect which did not bother

her one little bit. The defect was the reason she had gotten the expensive mug for such a reduced price. Sarah loved to go out shopping for lovely treasures that she could buy for less because they were overstocked, discontinued, slightly defective, or just plain on sale.

Sarah had never had much money to spend on luxuries, but if she could buy a beautiful item (possibly slightly flawed) for the same price as a plain one, she was all for that. As a result, her home had an abundance of brand-name colored floral cushions, rugs, and wall hangings in it. Sarah had an eye for color. She often wondered if she should have looked into being an interior decorator. Certain colors and patterns always fascinated her. Tilly had convinced Sarah that there was more job security for business secretaries than for interior decorators. She had encouraged Sarah to do some interior decorating on a personal level, just for themselves.

Sarah had loved making their small home into a peaceful haven for them both. Flowers were Sarah's favorite theme, but if she had more space with which to work, she would have incorporated gentle animals and all sorts of trees. Trees were interesting, especially the old and majestic ones, she always thought.

The dishes in the cupboard were also lovely--pale blue backgrounds with large sunflowers and summer flowers on the front. She felt good eating off of them every day. The sofa cushions were big and cozy in a variety of beautiful colors. There were mostly soft blue and green ones, with a few rose pink and lavender ones on the armchairs. The handmade rug in front of the sofa was a chunky cotton one made of sky blue, moss green, and soft pink fibers. It was warm to the touch and very pretty. Sarah and her mother had made fabric wall hangings in colors identical to that in the handmade rug. There were also a few beautiful pastel watercolor floral pictures on the walls, to compliment the rest of the room.

In the corner of the room was a pretty dresser, painted in robin's egg blue with white daisy handle pulls. Sarah had carefully stenciled rows of yellow flowers on the drawers. Inside the dresser was a multitude of lovely colored yarns and knitting needles jostled together. Two half-finished scarves were in the bottom drawer. One, she had been making for her mother, and the other for her landlady's birthday. Sarah supposed that she would finish her mother's scarf and wear it herself. She must remember to finish her landlady's scarf by next week so that she could give it to her when she paid her rent.

A long, tall, wooden bookcase against the wall held all of their favorite books and DVDs. Sarah and her mom had been collecting their favorite books for many years. These books were their most prized possessions. Tilly taught Sarah to wait to buy the early or first edition hardcovers of their favorite books. They used the public library to read the paperback copies of books that they wanted to read. The antique bookstore nearby was a fabulous place in which to buy their much-loved and sought-after books on their wish list. Over the last ten years, they had often bought their favorite books on an installment plan. The bookstore owner had become a good friend to Tilly and Sarah. He was always willing to set aside the books that they were looking for. They would make a down payment on the book of their choice, and he would agree to a monthly payment plan to pay for the book. He kept those books in his backroom, safe from other peoples' interest and grubby hands until Tilly or Sarah paid the final installment on the book. The pride of Sarah's collection was a first edition *Anne of Green Gables* hardcover. She had read Anne's story for the first time just after her father had died, and it was her very favorite book in the world. Anne's orphan status always made Sarah feel lucky that she still had her mom with her. Sarah loved Anne's dramatic way of speaking and dealing with her world. She also loved the author's interesting way of portraying any event. Lucy Maud Montgomery had captured Anne's unique character and the unconditional love that Matthew and Marilla Cuthbert grew to have for her in such poignant words. The way in which LM Montgomery exquisitely described the fictional Avonlea on Prince Edward Island made Sarah long to visit that lovely piece of eastern Canada. Sarah had eagerly read all of the books in the *Anne of Green Gables* series. She owned the first book, but the rest of the series was still on her wish list.

Their collection of DVDs was mostly made up of the classics, such as *Miracle on 34th Street, It's a Wonderful Life*, and other oldies, but goodies. They were much loved and had been watched a good many times. There was a small entertainment center in front of the couch which held the television, VCR, stereo equipment, and a bunch of CDs. Sarah's taste in music tended to be soft rock, instrumental guitar, harp, or piano music, and classical music.

On Monday, Sarah woke up early, excited about going to work. After her shower, she dressed carefully in her nice conservative outfit. Susan called her while she was eating her breakfast.

"Good morning, Sarah," said Susan, with a cheery voice. "Good luck on your first day at the new job. You'll be great--just be yourself. Call me when you get home tonight, and tell me all about your first day, ok?" she asked.

"Sure, Susan. Thanks for calling me to wish me good luck. I actually have a really good feeling about this job. I think that I am going to like it a lot," Sarah said confidently.

She made sure that she left in plenty of time to get to work. She parked in her designated spot. The parking lot had been thoroughly plowed, so Sarah did not have to trudge through a bunch of snow. Sarah thought that that was very considerate of Mr. Thompson.

She got to her desk fourteen minutes early. She found the door unlocked, which meant that Mr. Thompson was already there. She put her few treasures in her desk drawers since she did not see any other signs of personal effects anywhere in the office or waiting room. She put her floral notebook that claimed "Choose Joy" on the cover and its matching daisy pen inside her top desk drawer. Her favorite mug went into another drawer along with her purse, lightweight sweater, and the small framed picture of her mother. She took her lunch into the break room and found room for it in the fridge.

Within a few minutes, Mr. Thompson came out of his office. He paused next to her desk.

"Good morning, Miss Brewster," he said in a cheerful voice. "I hope that you had no difficulties getting here this morning?" he enquired.

"Good morning, Mr. Thompson," Sarah replied, with a smile in her voice. "Everything went very well for me this morning. Thank you for having the parking lot plowed. I was afraid that I might have to go through some snowbanks in order to get from my car into the office."

He looked at her thoughtfully and replied, "Oh, I always have the parking lot plowed. I would not want any of my employees to slip and fall on the ice or snow. By the way, remind me to give you the phone number of the company who does the plowing for us. I would like you to call them today and make their acquaintance. You will be the person who will be calling them from now on." Mr. Thompson spoke in a friendly voice. "Come into my office at 8:00 am with your notebook and pen so we can go over this morning's agenda. Thanks," he said with a nod and a smile. He left her and went into his office and shut the door quietly.

Sarah was kept busy for the next few minutes greeting her co-workers when they came in. They all introduced themselves to Sarah. She had a good memory, and she wrote down their names in her notebook when she had the chance to do so.

During her morning fifteen-minute coffee break with her co-workers, she casually asked them about their families and living situations. Sarah genuinely liked people and tried to find out what made them tick. Since she was an excellent listener, people tended to tell her things that they didn't tell other people-things like their birthdays, children's names and ages, and even wedding anniversaries. Sarah kept track of these things in her floral notebook. She loved to make and give small gifts to others and found that people enjoyed it when she remembered their birthdays with a small cake or other gift. She had learned that from her mother. Tilly Brewster had been so kind and always put other people first. She had taught Sarah how to knit many years ago. Sarah and Tilly had made small gifts, at one time or another, for just about every person they knew.

Tilly had recounted the day, shortly after her husband died, when she found a gift bag hanging on the knob outside their apartment door. Inside, she found Earl Grey tea, chocolates, and a small bag of Sarah's favorite cookies. There was a pretty card, written in lovely flowing script, stating that the gift was from a friend who knew Daniel and just wanted Tilly and Sarah to have a few treats. Tilly had accepted the gift, all the while wondering who it was from. The same gift showed up every month for about six months. Finally, Tilly caught the man and woman as they were putting it on the outside doorknob. She invited them into the apartment. They told her that they were Ben and Josie Olson and that Ben had worked at the nursery with Daniel. It seemed that Daniel often shared his lunch or snacks with Ben during their breaks. Daniel had told Ben all about his wonderful Tilly and sweet little Sarah. Ben had been new to the company and had relied on Daniel to teach him the ins and outs of the business. Daniel always shared whatever he had in his lunch box with Ben. After Daniel died, Ben found out where Tilly and Sarah were living, and he and Josie decided to leave them little treats, just because of his friendship with Daniel. Tilly was so pleased and happy to find out about their friendship. Daniel had never mentioned Ben or the way he shared his lunch and goodies with him. Ben and Josie became Tilly and Sarah's good friends from that day forward.

Ben was a lovable curmudgeon and Josie had a green thumb. She could grow anything. She always hummed while she worked. Josie often took young Sarah with her to visit Ben's workplace. It had the imaginative name of *All Things Bright and Beautiful.* Josie and Sarah spent many happy hours walking through the nursery, looking at flowers, and deciding what they would plant in Josie's garden in the springtime. Ben would grumble good-naturedly, although his brown eyes would twinkle. Sarah had been a bit wary of him to start with but soon realized that he was just a big cuddly teddy bear. His bark was definitely worse than his bite. Ben always allowed Josie and Sarah to purchase whatever seeds and bulbs they wanted. As a result, their garden was the most beautiful and varied in their neighborhood. They had come to Tilly's funeral and told Sarah to contact them if she needed anything at all, any time of the day or night.

Sarah heard from her co-workers that the boss was very hard-working and expected them all to work hard as well. Many of them thought that he was fair and very kind, but kind of aloof. None of his employees talked much about him, for they were loyal to him and the company. When they saw how very friendly and chatty Sarah was that first day, they advised her to keep her chattiness to herself. Sarah felt a little sad about that because she was a friendly girl who liked to talk about the great books, music, and movies that she had experienced, but now she found that she must keep these opinions to herself, at least while at work.

Sarah's first week on the job was spent finding out exactly how her boss liked things to be done. He met with her for about twenty minutes right away at 8:00 o'clock every morning. He gave her instructions for the days' work. Mr. Thompson was always courteous and pleasant with her, as he was with all of his employees. He didn't look over their shoulders, making sure that they were doing their work or not taking too much time on their breaks. Because of his trust in his employees, he had their respect and loyalty. Sarah really liked that about him. She had worked for other bosses who were always trying to micro-manage their staff. She liked to be given her daily work to do, and just get on with it. Because she was a quick learner and a very reliable secretary, she never had to ask anyone twice how to do something. She had a calm and efficient way of doing her work.

Paul was impressed with Sarah's quiet and pleasant manner and voice. She wrote down whatever she needed to do in her notebook and then got to work. He noticed that she was not a clock watcher. She had stayed fifteen or twenty minutes late the first few days to finish some work that could easily have been completed the next morning. She was a friendly girl but not chatty with him, the customers, or other employees. He liked that. He liked her simple dark skirts and white blouses, too. She did nothing to call attention to herself, but he could clearly see that she was a professional young lady with a calming presence about her.

Sarah had an hour break for lunch each day. When the weather was fine, she got into some comfortable walking shoes and took herself out to the nearby park to walk. She walked for thirty minutes, came back to the office, changed back into her good pumps, and hurriedly ate her usual lunch of a sandwich, fruit, and raw vegetables. She whisked herself to the restroom to make sure she was presentable and was back at her desk a few minutes before her hour was up. When the weather was too cold or rainy, Sarah went into the break room and ate her lunch with whomever was there. Because she was an amiable girl, she had no problems making friends. Her coworkers thought that Sarah was a very nice young lady. She really listened to what they wanted to talk about; she made them feel special.

One day, a few weeks after Sarah had begun to work for him, Mr. Thompson was in a bit of a panic because he could not find some papers that he needed for an upcoming meeting. He used his intercom to contact her.

"Miss Brewster, come in here, please. I need some help to find something," he said with a slight edge to his voice.

Sarah paused in her typing and went quietly into his office. She saw that his thick wavy hair was standing on end--*again*. She knew that he ran his hand through his hair when he was anxious or frustrated. She thought wryly to herself that it made him look like a very handsome little boy. She bit her lip to keep from grinning.

"Yes, Mr. Thompson, what are you looking for?" she asked him in her soft voice.

"I can't seem to locate the folder for the Phillips Company. Have you seen it?" he asked her.

Sarah calmly asked him, "No, I haven't seen it since yesterday. Do you remember the last time that you saw it?"

He stated in a vexed voice, "I worked on it last night at home, but I'm sure that I brought it in this morning. It's not in my briefcase. I've looked all over my desk and in the file cabinet. Will you please look elsewhere in the building for me?"

Sarah thought that she knew where it would be. She went straight to the copy machine that was in a small room outside Mr. Thompson's office. There it was, sitting open, next to the copy machine. She quickly picked it up and brought it into his office.

"Looking for this?" she asked in a friendly, but slightly sassy voice.

He looked at her and laughed, self-consciously. He grinned and said, "Don't tell me, I left it in the copy room, again, didn't I?"

Sarah smiled a big smile and said, "Yes. That will be my 'go-to' place from now on, whenever you can't find something. That makes two times, now, sir--*not that I'm counting.*"

Paul laughed ruefully and took the folder from her. "Thank you, Miss Brewster. I don't know what I would do without you."

Sarah smiled gently and went back to her desk. She enjoyed these little encounters with Mr. Thompson. He was such a quiet and professional man that you just didn't expect him to lose things and then joke about it when they were found. She wondered how she could tell him about his tousled hair. He would feel so embarrassed if he had an important visitor to his office and his hair was standing on end. Because it was so thick and wavy, it didn't fall back into place easily. He needed to comb it back into place. Perhaps she should just tell him. But she had only been his secretary for a few weeks, and he might think she was out of line if she told him about his messy hair. Personally, she thought that it made him look adorable. She would have to think some more about it.

THREE

Paul never saw Sarah upset or angry until one day, about a month after she had started to work for him. He was driving home around suppertime when he drove past a local supermarket. He noticed a small crowd looking at something in the large parking lot in front of the store. He decided to stop and take a look. He heard raised voices, one of them belonging to a woman. When he got closer, he was surprised to see his new secretary holding a scruffy-looking small dog. She was yelling at a couple of young boys.

"How dare you hit this little pup?" she shouted as she glared at a teenage boy of about fifteen years of age.

He was looking down at the ground, but he said belligerently, "Lady, it's my dog. It's no business of yours what I do with him. Stupid dog--he just peed all over my sack of groceries. My ma will be really mad at me for bringing home these stinky old groceries."

The younger boy looked fearfully at Sarah. "What are you gonna do, lady?" he asked her in a trembling voice. She looked so mad. He and his brother did not need any trouble. Their mom had a bad temper and might take it out on them if she heard about this trouble. There were also the soiled groceries to think about. There were a few other ladies standing around, just watching what was going on but saying nothing.

Paul recognized the two boys as regulars at the local food shelf that he volunteered at occasionally. He knew that they were not bad boys, just lacking in supervision and money.

Paul walked up to Miss Brewster and said in a friendly way, "Hello. Can I help?" He continued by asking, "What happened here? If you could start at the beginning, maybe we can work things out."

He paused to allow for Sarah's response, but the older boy quickly retorted, "Me and my brother were just putting the groceries in that basket on my bike. There were too many groceries to fit in my basket, so we had to put some in Billy's basket, too. 'Cuz Snuffles is too little to walk all the way home, I put him in my basket on top of the bag of groceries. Stupid dog... he just peed all over the bag! I guess I just got mad, so I hit him. This lady saw me do it and grabbed him. She yelled at us and won't give him back. Ma'll kill us for getting into trouble and bringing home those peed-on groceries." He looked quite angry and a little bit scared, as well.

Paul turned to Sarah, eyebrows raised, and asked her, "Well Miss Brewster, what is your interpretation of this story?" She cuddled the small dog and then looked at Paul.

"Mr. Thompson, it happened pretty much like that boy said. Only I will not allow anyone to hit an animal," she said fiercely.

"No, no, of course not," Paul told her in a soothing voice.

He looked at the boys and said, "Go through the groceries in the bag. Anything that is not ruined can be wiped off and taken home.

If there is anything that can't be used, take it out and throw it away." He added reassuringly, "We can buy some new groceries to replace them. Hurry up, now."

The fifteen-year-old started to comply with Paul's directions. He had a small pile of groceries that he would have to throw away. Paul sent the younger boy back into the store to ask someone there for some paper towels. One of the ladies in the crowd went with him to help out the situation. When the older boy had finished going through the groceries, he looked at Paul and said, "I don't have any more money for the new groceries, mister."

Paul looked at the boy and told him, "Not to worry, son. I think that I can spare the money so you can buy some new ones. Go back into the store and pick out the replacement groceries. I will be with you in a few minutes to pay for them. Meet me at the checkout stand."

The boy looked at his younger brother who was still wiping off some groceries. "You stay here, Billy. I can get the groceries. You watch Snuffles." He glared at Sarah once more before he ran back into the store.

Paul looked at Sarah and held out his arms. "I'll take Snuffles, now. I know who these boys are. I've met their mother. I will talk with them. I feel sure that they will never hit Snuffles again."

Sarah wasn't responding. The gentle face that he had quickly become accustomed to was set with determination.

"Will you trust me?" he asked her softly.

She looked deeply into his eyes and slowly nodded. "If you're sure, Mr. Thompson," she said gruffly. "I just get so angry when I see someone hurting an animal," she said with a firm voice.

"I understand," he told her quietly. He looked at the younger boy and told him to pick up all of the used paper towels and throw them in the trash can that was in the front of the store. The boy looked at Paul and Sarah and then ran to do what Paul told him to do. He came back quickly and held out his arms for the dog.

Paul held on to Snuffles, looked at Sarah, and said, "I've got this. Go ahead and go home. I'll talk with you tomorrow at the office, ok?"

Sarah looked like she wanted to argue but then just nodded and walked over to her car. Her car door was still open, groceries all over the front seat where she had tossed them when she had seen the boy hitting the dog. She moved the groceries over, got in, and drove slowly away.

The other ladies in the crowd also walked away, still without saying anything. It was a small diversion in their otherwise uneventful day. Paul, with Snuffles still safe in his arms, walked into the store. Billy stayed next to their bikes, keeping watch. Once in the store, Paul paid for the groceries. He walked the boy and his new groceries out to where his younger brother was waiting.

Paul said briskly, "Well, boys, what are we going to do about this? I've seen you and your mom at the food shelf. The next time I see her, I can either talk with her and tell her everything that happened, or we can learn from this and keep it among ourselves. What shall it be?"

The boys quickly looked at each other and said, "Keep it among ourselves!"

Paul gave them a stern look and told them, "You never take your frustrations or anger out on a defenseless animal--or anyone younger or smaller than yourself. That is not the way things are done. I don't want to ever see or hear that you have hit Snuffles or any animal, again. Do I make myself clear?" he asked the boys directly.

Both boys looked down at the ground for a minute and then chorused, "Yes, sir."

"Fine, then we understand each other," Paul told them. He handed Snuffles back to the older boy and looked at him. "What's your name, son? I know Billy's name but not yours," he spoke in a friendly voice.

Billy looked trustingly up at Paul and said, "His name is Johnny. Why?"

"You live near the St. Mary's Shelter on 2nd Street, don't you?" asked Paul, still in a friendly voice.

"Yeah," said Johnny. "Why?"

"Well, we have a weekly basketball game in the parking lot every Thursday night. Why don't you boys bring Snuffles and come over to play with us next week? The game starts at 6:30 pm. Come early so you can help us clear the parking lot of snow and slush. I will make sure that someone turns on the lights so that we can see and play the game." Paul told them. "I can make it to most of the games, but sometimes I have to miss them if I'm out of town. Right now, I'm planning to be there. I'd like to see what you guys can do on the court, okay?" he asked them.

"We'll ask Ma," said Johnny. "Thanks, mister."

Paul smiled at them and said, "My name is Paul Thompson. My friends just call me Paul. Now take those groceries home to your mother and keep your noses clean. See you next week, I hope."

He nodded at the boys and walked back to his car. He watched them get on their bikes and ride off. As he drove home, he grinned when he thought about Miss Brewster. Wow, what a feisty little gal she could be when she was riled up, he thought.

The next morning Paul talked with Sarah about the boys after they had gone through the day's agenda.

"Miss Brewster, I had a talk with Billy and Johnny. They're not bad kids. They just don't have enough money or supervision. They're going to start playing basketball with me and the kids from the homeless shelter. We have a pickup game on Thursday nights. They just need something constructive to do with their time. They love that dog. They don't want to lose him. I think that they were just afraid that their mother would be angry about the groceries. I intend to keep an eye on them. So, don't worry about little Snuffles anymore, ok?" he said to her.

Sarah just looked at him and thought about how nice he was to pay for the groceries and then help those boys out. "Okay. Thanks for telling me. But you know that I would do it again, if I saw it happening, again, right?" she asked him with a firm voice.

"Yes, I know, Miss Brewster--and that makes you a very nice person to know," he said with a smile in his voice.

One day Sarah took a phone call for Mr. Thompson from his fiancee. Her name was Belinda Rhodes, and she had a shrill and demanding voice. She demanded to speak to Mr. Thompson right away. When Sarah explained that he was on another call at that moment, Belinda became upset and wanted Sarah to go into his office and tell him that she was waiting to talk with him. Sarah explained in her calm way that he would be finished with his call quite soon and would call her right back. Belinda made a rude noise and slammed down the phone. Once Paul was off his phone call, Sarah went into his office and told him that Belinda had just called and wanted him to call her back immediately. Paul looked annoyed and thanked her.

Before she shut the door, he called after Sarah to come back for a moment.

He looked at her and said, "When I am on the phone, please just take down any incoming calls and numbers and bring them in after I am done with my call. You can tell by the red light on your phone system when I am using the phone. When it turns back to green, you may come in to give me any messages. You did well. I would have been upset if you would have interrupted my phone call. It was a business call. Only interrupt me when I receive an urgent call from my mother's doctor. I told him to call here if he needed to speak to me urgently. All other calls can wait until I am ready for them. Thank you, Miss Brewster." Sarah nodded and quietly left the room.

A few days later, a tall dark-haired young woman blew into Sarah's office. She was wearing a very stylish pantsuit and her hair and make-up were glamorously done.

She looked at Sarah and said, "My name is Belinda Rhodes. Tell Paul that his fiancee is here and is waiting to see him."

Sarah first looked to make sure that Mr. Thompson was not on the phone and then used the intercom to let him know about Belinda's visit. He said that he would be with her in five minutes and that Sarah should give Belinda some coffee.

Sarah offered coffee to Belinda, who looked down her nose at Sarah and said, "No, I'll just wait for Paul." Sarah invited Belinda to sit down in one of the comfortable chairs in the waiting room, but Belinda just stood there looking at her.

In her shrill voice, Belinda asked, "What is your name? You must be new because I don't remember seeing you before." Sarah told Belinda her name and that she had been working there for about five weeks. Belinda said sneeringly, "Well, I hope you are better at your job than that old battle-axe that Paul used to have working here." Sarah murmured quietly and looked down at the papers on her desk. She hoped that Mr. Thompson would hurry up and come out and take his Belinda away. She could not believe that such a nice, quiet man such as Paul Thompson would have asked a woman like Belinda Rhodes to marry him! Paul came out with his coat, took Belinda by the arm, and told Sarah that he would be back in two hours. He must have been frustrated because his hair was standing on end as he walked Belinda out of the door, Sarah thought, with a feeling of pity for him.

Sarah went on with her work, thinking about Paul and his fiancee. She felt sorry that Paul had to listen to Belinda's shrill and demanding voice. But maybe she acted differently with Paul when they were alone together. Sarah shook her head. She must stop thinking of her boss as Paul. She must think of him as Mr. Thompson, her boss, who was engaged to be married. She was starting to think about him too much, especially when she was alone at home. She knew by now that he was thirty-five years old, had two dogs, and lived in a nice old house on Rosemont Street. She knew that he had an ailing mother, whose doctor sometimes called Paul to update him on her progress. He had a brother named Joe, who was married and had two young sons. His sister, Kelly, was also married and had a little boy. Paul had asked her to send flowers to Kelly on her 30th birthday. Sarah had seen a few family pictures on the shelves in his office. He looked so happy holding one of his nephews and mugging for the camera. Paul was quiet in the office, but it seemed that he had a happy home life-- just like herself. She was a happy and chatty girl with her friends. It was just at the office that she was calm and quiet.

One evening, hours after his employees had left for the day, Paul looked up Sarah's address and drove himself to her home. He met

Sarah's landlady when he first knocked on the door. He told her who he was. She told him that Sarah lived on the top floor. As he walked up all of those steps, he wondered how she got all of her groceries and things all the way up there. He knocked on her door. No one answered. He listened closely and heard what he thought was the television and some music. He knocked again, louder, and finally, Sarah came to the door. She opened it and gave Paul a surprised stare.

"P-Please come in, Mr. Thompson," she stammered. He came into the room and looked around, surprised at how charming everything looked. The room smelled like hot buttered popcorn. He looked at Sarah and saw that her light brown hair was hanging loose, in a clean shining mass down her back, and she was wearing a pink soft fuzzy sweater, gray sweatpants, and flowered socks. Her large green eyes were glistening with tears, and her cheeks were pink with embarrassment.

He asked her with concern, "Are you all right?"

She blushed even more and said, "I am such a baby. I always cry at movies or books or music--anything that touches my heart. This movie is one of my favorites, but it makes me cry every time."

She led him into the living room area and asked him to sit down in the largest armchair. "Can I get you anything to drink?" she asked him.

"No," he said, "but I needed to drop off these forms for you to work on tomorrow. I will be out of town for three days, and I need these typed up and sent out as soon as you can get to them. They have top priority over anything else. I am sorry to bother you at home, though."

She took the papers and quickly looked through them to see if she understood what to do for all of them. They looked quite straight forward, and she replied that she would see that they were done tomorrow and sent out right away.

Paul made himself a little more comfortable in his chair and looked around him. He liked the pretty color theme and thought that she had decorated the small space cleverly and invitingly. He thought about how much the room suited Sarah. There was a large beautiful blue vase filled with fresh flowers on the table by the window. Flowers were Sarah's one weakness. It was her only extravagance. She would rather buy flowers each week than buy food. Paul looked at the three large photographs in their beautiful silver frames that graced the wall. One was a family picture; a gentle-looking young man and woman were standing behind a small girl with long light brown hair that was blowing around in the wind. Everyone was smiling. The girl was holding on to a large friendly-looking dog. The next picture was obviously Sarah and her mother. The woman was an older version of Sarah. They were both smiling huge smiles and looked so very happy. The other one was a picture of Sarah and a smiling young woman, with their arms around each other.

Paul pointed to the first picture and asked, "Your parents?"

"Yes," Sarah replied. "It was taken about a year before my dad died in a car accident. That was my dog, Wolfie. He died in the same accident as my dad. This next picture is of my mom and me in our favorite park almost three years ago, before she became really sick. The last picture is of my best friend, Susan. We were in school together. We had just come back from a friend's wedding, and we were so happy that day."

Paul did not say anything else. He got up to go and said, "Again, I am sorry that I disturbed your leisure time. I hope that you will have a chance to watch your movie at another time."

"Oh," she said candidly, "I can watch it whenever I want. It's a DVD. I felt in the mood to watch it tonight, but I don't mind that you came over."

As Paul left, he shut the door quietly behind him. As he walked to his car, he thought that Sarah was probably lonely. He knew how that felt because he often felt lonely himself.

FOUR

Sarah was liked by her co-workers because she was always there to give a helping hand, volunteering to do extra chores, handing out money for the charities that came to the office, and bringing them cakes or small gifts on their birthdays. One of the first things that she had done during her first week on the job was make up a spreadsheet with everyone's name and their birthdates. She had access to the personnel files and found out the information that she needed that she had not gleaned from her co-workers. She found out that Paul Thompson's birthday was only five days before her own--ten years before hers, though.

Mr. Thompson had seen the copy of the spreadsheet on her desk one day and had asked her to make him a copy, as well. She was glad to do that. She didn't know why he wanted it though. He never seemed to provide any birthday celebrations for his employees at work. What she didn't know was that he sent a check to each employee at their home address on their birthday. He did not want to make a big deal about his gift. His employees gladly accepted his generous checks and did not make a big deal about their birthdays either. The only one who made any outward show about birthdays was Sarah when she brought in their birthday cakes or other small gifts. She did not have any family left to make cakes or gifts for, so she made them for her co-workers, landlady, friends, and to give away at the church she belonged to. For Christmas, she knitted scarves, gloves, and other small items to give away. She found that even working full-time hours at the office, she still had plenty of time on her hands in her lonely little home. Of course, she had friends with whom she went out on occasion. She also saw Susan four or five times a month.

Sarah was invested in her job and always worked diligently at it. She was quick and professional at all times while she was dealing with clients, co-workers, and Mr. Thompson. She was friendly and calm during the little crises that came up from time to time, and totally trustworthy. Paul wondered how he had ever gotten along without her. Everyone who worked with Sarah liked her.

Because she was his secretary, Sarah was privy to all of Paul's charitable donations and other wonderful activities in the community. She knew that he gave money to at least a dozen organizations. He volunteered at the local food shelf, spent time at the homeless shelter in the area, played basketball on Thursday nights with underprivileged kids, and did a host of other admirable activities. She thought that he was perfect in every way, except for his engagement to the awful Belinda.

One evening she was in a baking mood. She made some of her luscious chocolate cupcakes with the thick frosting and sparkling glitter on top. Everyone that she gave them to said they tasted delicious and clamored for more. She hoped that Paul would allow her to offer them to the staff. They usually didn't have treats hanging around in the break room.

The next day Sarah knocked on Paul's door. She first checked her phone system to make sure that he was not on the phone.

"Come in," Paul called out, in response to her knock.

Sarah went in and stood by the door. "Do you have a minute, Mr. Thompson?" Sarah asked quietly.

He put down his pen and looked at her. "Sure, I can take a few minutes away from this tedious little letter that I am writing," he said with a smile. "Please come in and sit down. How can I help you?" he asked her.

Sarah sat a little self-consciously in the chair in front of his desk. She smiled uncertainly at him and asked, "Do you like chocolate cake, sir? I have only seen you eating salads. Maybe you don't like sweets?"

Paul shook his head and laughed, "Oh, I like sweets very much-- too much. That's why I need to eat salads for lunch. It keeps me honest, so to speak. Why do you ask?"

"Well, I like to bake, and I made some chocolate cupcakes last night. I brought some in, planning to put them in the break room for everyone. Before I did that, I wanted to ask your permission first. I also made a special one for you to say thank you. This is the nicest job that I have ever had." Sarah said earnestly.

Paul thought that she had made quite a speech. She usually did not have so much to say. "Thank you, I would love to try one of your cupcakes. I will have it later this afternoon when my lunch has worn off, and I start to feel hungry for supper," Paul said, with a big smile.

"Oh, good. I'll bring it in right away," Sarah said happily. She went back to her desk, took out a large chocolate cupcake, the elaborate frosting glistening with edible glitter, and brought it back into Paul's office. She set it on his desk and turned to leave.

"This looks too pretty to eat," Paul declared.

Sarah smiled and said, "Oh no, believe me, I have had several. It's very good. I think that you will enjoy it. Happy eating, sir," she said as she left the room. She gently closed the door and went back to her desk. She took the large plate of pretty cupcakes from her drawer and put them in the break room with a note that said "Enjoy. These are chocolate cupcakes--no nuts, just in case anyone is allergic to them. From Sarah."

That night, after everyone had left for the day, Paul walked through the main office where Sarah sat at her desk. He saw the fresh flower arrangement in its pretty vase on the side table. Sarah had been bringing in fresh flowers every week since the day he had told her that she may do so. He should really set some money aside to give her to buy them--flowers were expensive. He hadn't thought that having fresh flowers in the office and waiting area would make any difference to the room. Now he found himself looking for them each day as he walked through to go home. Their delicate scent and splash of color were just right for the room. Visitors to the office let him know that they enjoyed them, as well.

Paul was curious about Sarah and decided to look through her desk to see if he could find out anything more about her. He smiled when he saw her floral notebook and its accompanying daisy pen and the beautiful flowered mug. They were exactly the type of items that he would have guessed her to have in her desk. He looked at the picture of Sarah's mother. He felt sorry that she had to keep her treasures hidden in her desk. She obviously thought that he would not like it if she displayed them on top of her desk. He would have to think of a way to let her know that he wouldn't mind if she had a few tasteful articles on her desk-- without giving away the fact that he had looked in her desk drawers. As he drove home, he thought about Sarah's gift of the chocolate cupcake. He had really enjoyed it. Chocolate cupcakes were his favorite treat.

She had really made it beautiful with the swirling frosting and glitter. It was worthy of a bakery.

Sarah solved the problem of what to do about Mr. Thompson's stand-up hair. One day, she got to work earlier than usual. She took a round mirror and large comb into his office. She put them in the top drawer of his desk with a note saying, "These are for you to use before any important meeting. Sometimes your hair stands on end after you have run your hands through it. As your secretary, I just thought that I should tell you. Please do not feel offended. I would like to know if it was me." It was signed 'Miss Brewster'. She nervously worked at her desk that morning, wondering what Mr. Thompson would say when he saw them. She was unprepared for his bellow of laughter about an hour after he had started work that morning. She sat at her desk, fingers frozen on the keyboard, waiting for him to come out of his office.

The intercom buzzed. "Miss Brewster, please come in and see me for a moment," said an amused voice.

Sarah nervously went into his office and looked apprehensively at Mr. Thompson. "Yes, sir?" she asked him in a tentative voice.

"Please sit down, Miss Brewster," he invited, waving his hand towards the chair in front of his desk. She sat down, looking him squarely in the eye, "Here it comes," she thought to herself.

"I want to thank you for my gift this morning," he said, tongue in cheek. Sarah nodded, still looking at him. She waited for him to continue. "I appreciate your help in making sure that I am presentable at all times. I have had the habit for many years of running my hands through my hair. No one has ever told me that it makes my hair stand on end. All of those meetings, hundreds of them, and always with my hair in a mess. What they must have thought of me!" he groaned at the thought. "It took courage and a loyal heart to let me know about this issue. Thank you, again, Miss Brewster," he smiled as he spoke.

"You're welcome, Mr. Thompson," Sarah said, grateful that he was not angry with her. "As I said, I would want someone to tell me if my hair was messy when I was about to meet with important clients. You would tell me, wouldn't you, Mr. Thompson?" she asked him shyly.

He looked at her smooth shiny hair and pictured it loose and messy. He thought that it would be cute on her, but he said smoothly, "Of course, Miss Brewster. I promise to let you know if that ever happens. Thank you, again." Sarah left his office feeling very good about her talk with Mr. Thompson. He was a very nice man, she thought for the hundredth time.

It was the first week in June and Paul's birthday. He came into the office that Monday morning and found a luscious magnificently decorated chocolate cake on his desk. There was a cake knife resting on top of a Happy Birthday paper plate. There was a wonderful birthday card standing up next to it. On the card was a great scene of a tall dark-haired man walking two black dogs along a sunny gravel road. It could have been made specifically for him. Sarah had written, "Happy Birthday, Mr. Thompson. I hope you have the best day ever." It was simply signed 'Miss Brewster'. Paul smiled at the card and looked closely at the cake. It looked like it had come from an exclusive bakery, but he was sure that Miss Brewster had made it herself. He walked back to her desk and thanked her for it.

She smiled at him and told him, "It was no trouble. I love to bake. You told me that you liked chocolate cake, so I figured that you would enjoy this. Maybe you can share it with Ms. Rhodes or your family tonight. Are you planning to do anything special this evening?" she asked him, with her friendly voice.

"Yes, I have plans for this evening. I would really like to share this wonderful cake with everyone here today. I'm sure to have another cake this evening. Will you get some plates, forks, and napkins ready? I will just cut this into small pieces and leave it in the break room for everyone to enjoy. But first, I am going to take a big piece for myself. I'll have it with my coffee at 10:00 this morning. Make sure you get a piece for yourself, Miss Brewster." he said comfortably.

Paul thought about the cake that evening while he was out with Belinda. She had given him no card or gift. In fact, she had demanded that he take her out to eat. If Belinda knew that it was his birthday, she gave no sign of it. Paul sighed when he thought about how selfish Belinda could be. Just once he would like it if she asked him what he wanted to do instead of always demanding that they do what she wanted to do. He compared Sarah's sweet and thoughtful gift to Belinda's egocentric demands and found Belinda definitely lacking in any thoughtfulness or basic niceness. He felt upset with himself for finding Belinda so annoying and thoughtless. He had, after all, asked her to marry him. True, that had been more than two years ago, but now he was appalled at his reluctance to think about their future life together. He was no longer satisfied with his engagement to Belinda. He wished that she was different, sweeter, someone more like Sarah Brewster.

Because of Sarah's birthday spreadsheet, Paul knew that Sarah's twenty-sixth birthday was on Friday, just five days after his own birthday. He usually just sent his employees a check to their home addresses. But as he got out his checkbook, he wondered if Sarah would think that a check was a little impersonal. She seemed like the type of person who would enjoy a more personal gift. He knew that she loved flowers, so he decided to get her a beautifully illustrated hardcover book about North American flora and fauna. He had seen such a book at the bookstore in the mall when he had gone there with his sister last weekend. He went back to the mall and thankfully they still had the book in stock. He bought it and stuffed a crisp fifty-dollar bill inside as a bookmark. Then he had the store wrap it in beautiful paper that was covered in colorful balloons. He smiled when he thought about her reaction to the book. He was pretty sure that she would love it. He went to the card shop and found a sweet card that was perfect for Sarah. He planned to watch her face when she opened her gift.

Sarah saw the bright gift on her desk when she came into the office on Friday. Grinning hugely, she wondered who had left her a gift. No one did much regarding birthdays at this office. She did not notice Paul's door opening quietly, nor him standing there watching her. Sarah carefully opened the card that was attached. It was a sweet picture of a small girl with long light brown hair kneeling in a field of flowers picking a bunch of white daisies. It could have been Sarah as a toddler. She was so pleased with the card. She opened it up and read out loud, "To Sarah Brewster, I hope that you get all of the flowers that you could ever wish for on your birthday." It was signed by Paul Thompson. She opened her gift and saw the hardcover book. She had seen it at the store and had admired it. When she saw the fifty-dollar bookmark, her eyebrows raised in surprise. Sarah was very touched and pleased by her gift. She looked up and saw Paul watching her from his office doorway. He had a gentle smile on his face while he watched a host of expressions pass over her face. They ranged from happiness to surprise to quiet contentment.

She set the book down and walked over to Mr. Thompson. Because, for her whole life, she had hugged and kissed her family and friends after receiving a gift, she did not even stop to think of the inappropriateness of it, but she reached up and hugged Mr. Thompson and kissed his cheek. She stopped and blushed as soon as she realized what she was doing.

"I am so sorry, Mr. Thompson," she said in a flustered voice.

Paul grinned widely and said, "Think nothing of it, Miss Brewster. I am very glad that you are pleased with your present. I hope that you don't already have that book," he queried.

"No, but I have seen it and admired it at the store. I'm going to have such a good time looking through it at home," she said happily.

"Good, good," he said placidly. Sarah was still a bit embarrassed by her actions, but Mr. Thompson seemed to be reacting with grace. He did not seem the least bit annoyed or upset by her impulsive hug and kiss for him. Sarah felt relieved and smiled shyly at him before going back to her desk.

That afternoon, as she was packing up to go home, Paul came out of his office and said to her, "Again, a happy birthday to you, Miss Brewster. Do you have plans for this evening?"

She smiled and said, "Oh yes, my best friend, Susan, is taking me out for lasagna tonight. We both love it. I'll bet that she will be jealous of my book. She likes that kind of book, as well."

Paul smiled and nodded and told her good night in a friendly voice. She responded in kind, and they walked out to the car park together in friendly silence. Paul got in and waved to her when he pulled past her little car. Sarah gave him a great big smile and waved back. She couldn't wait to tell Susan all about her day. As Paul drove himself home, he thought about Sarah and her reaction to his gift. It had been a pleasant surprise to him when she hugged him and kissed his cheek. He had really enjoyed them. She was such a warm-hearted little thing, he thought.

Belinda had never reacted that way when he had given her a gift. She tended to take gifts for granted and was often not very excited about what she received. He knew for a fact that she returned some of his gifts because she had asked him for the receipts. She had laughingly told him that she was fussy and liked what she liked. She had told him not to worry because nobody got her gifts that she liked. She had been exchanging her parents' gifts for most of her life. They usually only give her money these days. She hoped that he would not be angry if she returned his gift for the money or for something that she liked better. That had been about the time when he had started giving her only flowers whenever he wanted to buy her a gift. He also spent a pretty penny taking her out to all of the most popular and exclusive places to dine and dance. Sarah Brewster's response had been much more satisfying to him. Here was a woman who actually liked the gifts that he bought. He frowned at himself. He found himself comparing Belinda and Sarah much too often these days. It seemed like Sarah always came out on top. Now what did that say about Belinda?

CHAPTER
FIVE

It was Sunday, again. Sarah's routine very rarely changed from week to week. After a leisurely breakfast, she drove to the church that she had attended her whole life--first with her mom and dad, then with just her mom, and now by herself. She felt comforted by the sameness she always felt whenever she walked into the old building. She knew most of the members of the parish, as well as the priests. Her dad and mom were buried side by side in the adjoining cemetery. After mass, she would stop and talk briefly with friends, and then make her way to the cemetery with her gift of flowers in her hands. She would stop and chat with old friends of her parents who had long since taken their place in the cemetery. Then she would sit on her mother's grave, placing the flowers equally between her parents' graves. When the weather was nice, she would often while away an hour just chatting with her mom and dad. She told them all about her week--the good things and the bad things. She always felt refreshed after she left them. She often told them how appreciative she was to have them to talk to.

After she left her parents, Sarah would drive to the Royal Gardens, which was a beautiful showplace of flower gardens, walking paths, and open grassy areas. She knew quite a few of the regulars who walked their dogs or just wanted to lose themselves among the lovely scented acres. Today, Sarah ran into her friend, Clara Burke, sitting on one of the benches in a large grassy area. Her sweet little pup was straining on his leash next to her on the bench. Sarah greeted her friend with a hug and a caress for the puppy.

"How is Rip doing?' Sarah asked.

"Oh, he is as feisty as ever. If I didn't have this leash on him, he would be gone in a flash," Clara chuckled. They settled down for a nice gossip.

Paul, holding the leashes of his two black labs, saw Sarah while he was quite a distance away. He saw her laughing and chatting with the woman and her dog. Sarah looked so pretty, with her long shiny hair loose and gleaming in the sun. Her skirt and top were also pretty and feminine. He just stared at her. She looked so different from the way she looked in the office every day. He had rarely seen her talking so much and laughing at the office. As he came near to them, Sarah saw him and smiled up at him.

"Oh, Mr. Thompson, I didn't know that you came here to walk your dogs," she said.

He smiled down at her and said, "I heard about this place from someone, and I wanted to check it out. My dogs, Mutt and Jeff, like to take me for a long walk on the weekends."

He looked at Clara and was about to speak, when Sarah said, "Mr. Thompson, this is my friend Clara, and her little dog, Rip." She looked at Clara and asked, "Clara, is it okay if they sit down and chat for a while?"

Clara said, "The more the merrier, I always say." Paul sat down, still holding the dogs' leashes tightly in his hands.

Sarah looked at them and said, "Oh, they are so beautiful. May I stroke them, please?"

Paul looked pleased, and said, "Sure, they won't hurt you. Do you like dogs, Sarah?"

She smiled and said, "Oh yes, I love dogs. I used to have my own dog when I was little. When he and Daddy died, we had to go and live in an apartment. There has not been room for a dog ever since then." She looked sad for a moment, and then smiled and reached out to pet Rip. "I get to see plenty of dogs now, though. Lots of my friends have dogs. Someday, I will live somewhere where I can have them again."

Paul didn't know what to say, so he turned to Clara and asked, "Why is your puppy called Rip?"

Both Sarah and Clara burst out laughing. Clara told Paul how she had acquired Rip. She related the Christmas Eve story to him. Paul laughed outright after Clara had finished her story. Sarah quietly thought about the fact that Paul had called her Sarah, instead of Miss Brewster. She felt that it meant that they were starting to become friends. She would still have to call him Mr. Thompson because he was her boss, but the fact that he had unconsciously called her Sarah, made him seem a little bit more approachable.

Paul started to enjoy himself. He listened to Sarah chattering away with Clara. He never knew Sarah could be like that. Sarah had a very warm laugh. She stroked the dogs' heads while she talked. They were all straining to get closer to her. He thought about Belinda then. Belinda hated dogs. She never came out walking with them. Paul usually walked his dogs by himself, unless he was at his brother's house. Joe or his boys were always up for a walk or romp with the dogs. He found out that Sarah spent most Sunday afternoons at the Royal Gardens when the weather was nice. He asked them if he could see them again next week. They made a tentative date to meet at 3:00 pm next Sunday. As he walked away, Paul felt pleased and looked forward to their next meeting.

Over the next few weeks, Paul met Sarah and, quite often, Clara and Rip, by the benches in the grassy acres at the Royal Gardens. One Sunday he asked Clara how she had gotten to know Sarah. Clara talked about the early years when Sarah and her mom had strolled around the gardens and paths every Sunday. Clara and her beloved husband, Bob, used to walk their husky on Sundays, too. They met one day and liked each other immediately. After that, they had made a habit of joining forces on the grassy areas or sitting on the benches, just talking. As the years went by, Sarah and her mom's friendship helped Clara deal with the sudden unbearable loss of her beloved husband after he died from a heart attack. A few years after that, they were there for her when her husky died. Then, in turn, she had helped Sarah deal with Mrs. Brewster's slow and painful illness, and finally, her death. They had a true friendship, having lasted through many years and many tears. They had also managed to laugh quite a lot, as well. Paul thought that they were lucky to have each other. He wished that he had someone like that in his life, someone who just accepted him for his true self--someone who never judged him or expected things from him. Sarah and Clara had no expectations of each other but were just happy to spend time together whenever it worked out for them.

He cherished his times with them, especially with Sarah. Sunday was becoming the best day of the week for Paul. He started to see how enchanting Sarah was. She was always happy, friendly, caring, and so pretty and feminine. He learned that her motto in life was "Choose Joy". She lived every day in a joy-filled way. He smiled whenever he thought about his emerging friendship with the sunny and delightful Sarah. She sometimes talked about her parents when she was at the Royal Gardens. She told Paul that her father's pet name for her was Sunshine. Paul thought how absolutely perfect that name was for her. She liked the nickname so much but there was no one left in her life who could legitimately call her Sunshine--with the possible exception of Ben and Josie. Sarah had mentioned them by name a few times when she had been with Clara, Rip, Paul, and his dogs.

Paul was going to have to do something about Belinda. Why had he ever thought to ask her to marry him? He knew it was because he was getting older and wanted to marry and have a family. He had thought that Belinda wanted that, too. Before he proposed to her she had said that she wanted a husband and family. However, the longer their engagement went on, the more he found that they had little in common anymore. They had been engaged for two years. He found out that Belinda just wanted to party and go out on the town. She now said that she was not interested in having any children, and that was something that he wanted very much. Belinda was harsh in her judgement of anyone whom she considered to be inferior to herself. Because she grew up always having enough money, she was intolerant of those who had to scrape up a living. She abhorred the fact that Paul donated money to, and spent quite a lot of time at, the local food shelf at St. Mary's Shelter. He had invited her several times to watch his Thursday night basketball games with the kids from the shelter. She had shrieked and told him that she did not ever plan to go near them. She thought that the kids were dirty and probably would try to steal from her, little convicts that she thought they were. He explained that they were just kids, like any other kids. She told him never to invite her again. Paul stopped talking with her about any of his community outreach activities. He had a good life and great childhood, and he just wanted to give back to the community. He really enjoyed his times playing basketball with the kids and volunteering at the food shelf. Paul doubted that Belinda loved him, and now, after getting to know Sarah better, he realized that he could not spend the rest of his life without love.

He found himself falling in love with Sarah, for all the delightful things she was. She was so whimsical and happy. She had a wonderful sense of humor. Her laugh was enough to make him smile, every time. He was very careful not to show his true feelings for her. He would have to talk with Belinda and get her to release him from their engagement before he could even think about asking Sarah out on a date. He could not be unfair to either Belinda or Sarah. There were a few times when he could swear that he saw something like a deep friendship--dare he hope to think, maybe even love--in Sarah's eyes when she smiled at him. She smiled at him so much more when they were away from the office. At the office, she was always professional and coolly friendly. He guessed that that was the way it should be, too.

One Sunday evening while Paul was sitting in his most comfortable leather armchair in his living room, the doorbell rang. He had just come in from a long walk with his dogs. They were now laying on either side of his chair, resting. He had had a lovely afternoon at the Royal Garden. He had met up with Clara, Rip, and Sarah. Clara and Rip had stayed around for only an hour before they had to go. Apparently, Clara's daughter and grandchildren were visiting her that evening. Paul and Sarah and his dogs had wandered around the fragrant paths at the Royal Garden, talking about work and anything else they thought of. It had been such a lovely afternoon and early evening. Sarah had been wearing a pretty sundress and her hair was loose. It blew all around in the light breeze while they walked. She kept trying to subdue it, but Paul enjoyed looking at its messy brightness. His hands itched to touch it--gather it up and feel its warm silky length. Sarah kept laughing gently about everything. He had laid himself out to be as charming and humorous as he could be. He had grabbed her hand as they walked along. She had looked surprised but hadn't pulled away. Paul had felt a very deep contentment and had enjoyed himself more than he had for quite a long time. He knew by now that he loved Sarah. It was so pleasant to spend time with her. He wondered if he would ever get to tell her about his love for her. As he sat daydreaming about his lovely day, he realized that the doorbell rang several times. He went to the door and found Belinda there. She was all dressed up in a slinky black dress, lots of gold jewelry, and high heels.

"I thought that I would come and get you, darling," Belinda said with her shrill voice. "Everyone is going to the opening of that new dance club downtown. Get yourself dressed up and take me there, Paul," Belinda demanded.

Paul brought her into the room and sat her down. "I am just getting ready to have an early night," Paul told her quietly.

"What an old fuddy-duddy you are becoming, darling," Belinda pouted. "It has been weeks since you took me anywhere decent. You always want me to sit around here, doing nothing. I get bored with doing that. I want to have some fun for once. Come on, darling, take me out tonight," she pleaded.

Paul wearily got up and asked her to give him ten minutes to change. He saw her triumphant expression as he turned to go upstairs to his bedroom. He came down ten minutes later in a smart-looking suit, silk shirt, and tie. He spent a few minutes putting his dogs to bed, and then they left. Paul did his best to be the type of escort that Belinda wanted. He smiled and danced, but his heart was longing to go home and go to bed. He had a long day planned for the next day. Mondays were always busier than other days because things happened over the weekend that needed to be dealt with on the first day back at work. Belinda kept him out until the wee hours of the morning. When he finally drove her back to his house to pick up her car, she bubbled over with talk about the wonderful time that she had had that night. As Paul leaned over to kiss her goodnight, Belinda turned her head so that his kiss fell onto her cheek. She apparently did not want him to kiss her, he thought. He said goodnight and told her to drive home carefully. Belinda was still talking about the evening when she drove away. Paul shook his head as he tiredly walked into his house and locked up. The difference between his lovely afternoon and the tedious time he had had at the dance club was uppermost in his mind as he got himself ready to go to bed. His tired head hit the pillow, and he was out like a light.

The next morning at work Paul was a little grumpy because he was tired and unhappy with his relationship with Belinda. He knew that he needed to talk with her and end their engagement, but he was loath to hurt her. It actually hurt his heart a little to see Sarah, so calm and friendly sitting at her desk. She smiled her gentle smile at him as she wished him good morning. He wanted to go to her and hug her, but he could never do that because of Belinda. He said his good morning quietly and hurried to his office. He didn't intend to do so but accidentally slammed his office door as he closed it. Sarah looked at his door, round-eyed, and wondered what had happened to Paul. He was usually the most courteous of men. She had never heard him slam his door before.

She gave him a few minutes before knocking on the door at 8:00 am, ready to go over the day. "Come in," she heard him say testily. Sarah calmly walked into the room and sat herself down in her usual chair, waiting for him to speak. He looked at Sarah sitting there so calmly and patiently. He thought, as always, that she was such a gentle-looking and pretty young woman.

"I'm sorry if I am out of sorts this morning. I haven't had much sleep," he told her grumpily.

"No problem, Mr. Thompson," she said briskly. "Everyone has bad days once in a while. Think nothing of it," she said, reassuringly.

"Thank you, Sarah," he said with a sigh. "Do you ever have one of those days?" he asked her.

"Oh, sure," she said in a friendly voice. "Now, what do you need me to do this morning, sir?" she asked him.

He pulled himself together and gave her instructions for the day. She left, closing the door softly as she went back to her desk. Paul sighed, again, and shook his head. If Sarah was going to continue working for him, he was going to have to get his feelings under control. The sooner he broke his engagement with Belinda, the better, he thought, with a grimace. It ended up being a very long and tiring day for Paul. He was glad to go home to his dogs and Mrs. Kennedy's good meal.

That next Saturday evening, Paul and Belinda ran into Sarah and her date at a local seafood restaurant. Sarah was dining with her good friend, Bruce. Like herself, he was a member of the "Young Adults Club" that their church sponsored. Bruce and Sarah were casually friendly. Neither one wanted a serious relationship. They enjoyed going out occasionally when one or the other needed to attend a function or wanted to celebrate a birthday or other special event. They both casually dated other members of their "Young Adults" group, too. Tonight, was Bruce's 27th birthday, and he felt like celebrating a bit with someone. Sarah was his favorite date because she was sweet and friendly, as well as being a pretty girl. Because they both had a good sense of humor, they laughed a lot when they were together. Both of their families had tried to get them together more often and wondered why they couldn't fall in love with each other. They were puzzled about it, themselves. But, for whatever the reason, they just remained good buddies, who both liked to occasionally spend some time together.

Paul was surprised to see Sarah with a young man. For some reason, he had never thought about Sarah dating anyone. He thought of her as a homebody, preferring to spend her evenings at home watching old movies or reading and listening to music. He already knew that she liked to knit. He could picture her, knitting something, listening to classical music, while eating some hot buttered popcorn. Now he had to face the fact that she enjoyed dating young men. They looked like they were having a really good time, too. The sound of their infectious laughter, which wafted over to them quite often, made his uncomfortable silences with Belinda seem even longer. Belinda was not much of a conversationalist when they went out to eat. She only really sparkled when she was the center of attention at a party with her friends. As he and Belinda were leaving the restaurant, they walked past Sarah's table. Paul stopped a moment to say hello to them.

He introduced Belinda to Sarah, saying, "Belinda, you remember my secretary, Sarah Brewster, don't you?" Belinda abruptly nodded her head but said nothing.

Sarah smiled at them and introduced Bruce to them. "Bruce, this is my boss, Mr. Thompson, and his fiancee, Belinda Rhodes. Mr. Thompson, this is my friend, Bruce."

Paul was a bit frustrated that Sarah did not say anything more about Bruce. Who was he, and how involved was he with Sarah? They all talked casually for another thirty seconds before Paul and Belinda took their leave. Belinda sat there sulking in the car because Paul had told her that he couldn't go with her to a party later that evening. He had an important meeting coming up on Monday, and he still had to prepare for it. He dropped her off at her home with a wave and told her that he would call her later next week. He told her to take care and have fun at the party. She wouldn't even look at him or talk to him. She just flounced out of the car and slammed the door. Paul thought about Sarah and Bruce as he drove to his home. He admitted to himself that he was feeling jealous about Sarah being on a date with Bruce. He reminded himself that he had no right to feel that way. Sarah could date anyone she wanted. Until he broke off his engagement with Belinda, he had no right to be jealous of another man.

The next afternoon, Paul ran into Sarah, Clara, and Rip at the Royal Gardens. They were sitting there, chatting, on a bench in the grassy area. Paul's two dogs raced over to see their friend, Rip. Poor little Rip had a large bandage on the side of his head where he was severely scratched from tangling with a rose bush. Sarah was cuddling him and crooning softly to him. Paul thought that she was so sweet. He was so pleased that she liked dogs. If, by some miracle, they ever got together, he knew that she would love Mutt and Jeff as much as he did. His dogs were a big and important part of his life.

They all talked for half an hour before Clara reluctantly said that she wanted to get little Rip home and bathe his wound. Sarah hugged both Clara and Rip goodbye. She looked shyly at Paul and asked, "Have you taken Mutt and Jeff for their walk, yet, or are you about to leave to go home, Mr. Thompson?"

Paul said in a half-laugh, "I think it's time that you called me Paul, outside of the office. After all, we know each other pretty well, by now. I have called you Sarah for some time now."

Sarah looked quizzically at him. "Do you really want me to call you Paul? I feel that it is impertinent to call your boss by his Christian name."

"Well, you may still call me Mr. Thompson at work, but I think we can safely say that we are friends outside of work, can't you?" he asked.

They walked around the beautiful grounds for an hour, talking and laughing about the comical things that Paul's nephews did the last time he had seen them. His brother's two young sons loved Paul's dogs and usually wrestled with them in their grassy backyard. Paul generally spent one weekend a month at his brother's house. His brother, Joe, usually invited their sister, Kelly, and her husband and son to spend the day with them, as well. When their mother was feeling fine, Paul picked her up and brought her over, too. They were a close family, and they loved to spend their free time together. Paul adored his three nephews. Kelly's little boy was only five, whereas Joe's two sons were seven and eight years old. Paul was their beloved uncle, and he treated them with love and care. Being with his nephews made him long for his own children, someday. He was patient and kind with children.

Paul didn't want their time together to be over, so he asked Sarah, "Would you like to get some pizza for supper? I am just in the mood for some of that really cheesy gooey pizza that they have advertised at that new pizza joint by the office. Have you been there, yet? It's supposed to be very good. We can talk about some things I will need you to do tomorrow at the office. Consider it a working supper, as it were." He smiled down at Sarah.

She smiled back at him and said, "Thank you, Paul. I would like that very much. I should tidy up, first, though."

He looked at his dogs and said, "I need to take these guys home, first. Why don't you follow me home? You can tidy up at my house while I give them their supper. Okay?"

Paul had a beautiful old house with a large manicured lawn and a garden peeping out around the corner of the house. Sarah wanted to go and see his garden more than anything, but she wondered if she would ever see it.

Inside the house, he led her to a large bathroom on the main floor, where she could tidy up. He told her that it would take about ten minutes to feed his dogs. It only took her a few minutes to wash her face and comb her hair, so she decided to look around. She went into the living room. It looked very comfortable, with a large leather couch and comfortable-looking armchairs in front of a large entertainment center. There was a wonderful old brick fireplace against the wall.

"What a wonderful place to snuggle up on a cold winter's evening," she said out loud.

"Oh, it is. This is my favorite place to be in the winter," Paul said from the doorway. Sarah whipped around, blushing furiously because he caught her snooping in his house.

He grinned at her and said, "I will take you on a tour sometime if you want. Only right now, I am so hungry that I can hardly wait for that pizza. Let's go, okay?"

Sarah said, "I'm sorry that I was snooping. I have always wondered what your house looked like."

Paul caught her by the arm and urged her out the door. "No problem, I'm sure you will have the chance to see it another time."

They had a wonderful time at the pizza joint. They talked and laughed, finding that they had a great deal in common. She asked him about his garden, and he told her that he loved to potter around in it on his free weekends. She asked if she could see it sometime, and he was happy to tell her that he would enjoy showing it to her. They left the pizza joint on a happy note, well satisfied with each other's company.

CHAPTER
SIX

Every July, Paul hosted a company picnic. He and his secretary spent several weeks planning every small detail. The last few years, his secretary wanted them to do fewer physical activities and do more sitting around in comfortable chairs talking and playing card games while a few of the men grilled the steak and vegetables. She was an older woman, who did not enjoy all of the physical activities that sometimes were prevalent at picnics. Paul, who enjoyed running around and playing physical games, hoped that Sarah was of like mind.

Paul and Sarah decided to meet at a coffee house after work one day in late June to start the preliminary discussions about this years' picnic. Paul had planned the past nine picnics with his secretary. He told Sarah about the themes and the highlights of each of the picnics. He laughed when he told her about the picnic that they had to celebrate his first year in business. It had been a lean year. None of them had made much money that year. The employees had all agreed to bring the food and games, a kind of potluck. Funnily enough, that had been one of his favorite picnics of all time. As he grew more profitable each year, the picnics became more substantial. After his fifth picnic, he decided to start handing out company gifts to his employees at the picnics. It had proved to be so satisfying, that he had continued to make that a priority at subsequent picnics.

Sarah enjoyed Paul's upbeat and good-natured manner while they planned the upcoming picnic. At the office, Paul was quiet and professional at all times, like herself. When away from the office, their true colors came out. They both were highly creative and were always thinking of ways to make life a bit better for someone else. It had been a banner year, he confided. He wanted to think of some great gifts to give his employees as a way of showing his thanks and appreciation for all of their excellent work. He was interested in any ideas that Sarah could come up with, however grand.

After that first meeting, in which Paul had outlined past picnics, Sarah had a lot to think about. She, with her friendly conversation in the break room, slyly asked her co-workers what they prized and would get for themselves if they had unlimited funds at their disposal. Back at her desk, Sarah got out her trusty notebook and daisy pen and made notes about all she had discovered from them. She searched the internet and catalogs for merchandise and the cost of everything she had on her list. She brought her notebook and her information to the next meeting with Paul. They had a hilarious time, making grandiose suggestions and plans for the upcoming picnic. Paul wanted a picnic extraordinaire.

After an especially funny anecdote, Paul just sat and looked at Sarah. Her eyes were bright and smiling, her cheeks flushed a pretty pink, and her hair was hanging in a shining mess over her shoulders. She had an endearing habit of running her fingers through her long locks while she was writing and thinking. This caused her hair to get a little messy. Paul thought at that moment that she was the most beautiful girl that he had ever seen. He loved her; she was everything he had ever wanted in a wife. He wanted to tell her so, but he was afraid to let her see how he felt about her. He was still not free of Belinda, and it would not be fair to lead Sarah on with his words or actions. He smiled at her, instead, and said they should probably wrap it up for the night. He had to get home and take the dogs for a walk. Sarah, ever conscious of his moods, felt him distancing himself from her. She wondered what she had said or done to make him withdraw into himself like that. She quietly agreed, picked up her notebook and pen, and got up to go. Paul paid the modest bill for their snacks and beverages and walked her out to her car. He grabbed her hand for a second, squeezed it, quietly thanked her for her help, and said good night. They both drove away, feeling saddened that their nice evening had ended in such a way.

Sarah now knew, without any doubt at all, that she was totally in love with Paul. She thought about him every day. It was heaven to be in his company every day at work. Because of his engagement to Belinda, Sarah could never let Paul see how she felt about him. She would have to be extremely careful to be just friendly and helpful to him at work and also when they happened to meet outside of work. This was the best job that she had ever had, even discounting Paul. She did not want to leave and start over somewhere else. If only he was not engaged to Belinda…

The day of the picnic dawned clear and sunny. It was going to be a hot day. Sarah was glad that it was Saturday and there was nothing for her to do except to see that the picnic ran smoothly. She was expecting Paul to come over at noon to pick up the employee gifts and assorted other items that they would need at the picnic. They had decided to use a catering service for the meal. The service would set up the tents, tables and chairs, as well as provide the massive grills for grilling the meat. Pretty much everyone liked steaks, so they had decided to serve grilled steaks, shrimp, and chicken, a variety of vegetables that could go on the grill, huge bowls of salads with every topping available, melon boats filled with watermelon, cantaloupe, grapes, raspberries, and blueberries, and corn on the cob, dripping with melted butter. There were to be three or four types of desserts, including a large decorated sheet cake congratulating them all on a wonderful year. There would be a variety of beverages to suit everyone's tastes.

They were both going to take their own cars to the park. The back seat of Paul's car would already be half-filled by Mutt and Jeff, who were to attend the picnic with him. Sarah looked at the large brightly wrapped gifts that she had wrapped last night. They had decided that each employee would receive a voucher for a weekend getaway at one of the hotels in town, at company expense. Sarah put together elegant baskets which included the vouchers in a glossy envelope, a small bottle of champagne, decadent chocolates, and a few small items specific to their individual interests and tastes. She couldn't wait to see their faces when they opened their gifts. Sarah and her co-workers had met secretly and decided on a terrific gift for Paul. He would be bringing her gift with him in his car. She put all of the others' gifts in her car, along with some of the props they would need for their activities.

Paul arrived a little early, so they sat down in her comfortable shabby armchairs to go over all of the details for the day. Sarah got up to check something in her kitchen. Paul watched her go and thought how pretty she looked in her pink sundress. He sat there, daydreaming about Sarah until she came back. She came back into the room and asked him if he was ready to check off each item on her list to make sure they had everything they needed. She needed to repeat herself several times before he came out of his reverie.

"Oh, sorry, I was just wondering if we missed anything," Paul said sheepishly.

"Are you kidding, we have every detail thought out and accounted for," Sarah said, laughingly. "Now let's get this show on the road, buster!" she forcibly stated. Paul laughed as they left her apartment, laden down with gifts and other paraphernalia.

This year, the picnic was to be held at the big community park on the edge of town. The park had everything that a picnicker could want. There were trails to walk on, beach volleyball and badminton set up, a playground for the little ones, a tennis court, a swimming pool, an ice cream and slushy stand, soccer fields, and wide-open areas of soft green grass, just perfect for laying down on or chasing around on. In their cars, Paul and Sarah had every type of racquet, balls, floating devices, and towels that they could think of. The employees just needed to show up, by themselves, or with any family members that wanted to come along. It was supposed to be a day just for fun and camaraderie.

Sarah kept busy, making sure that everyone was having a good time. It was great to see her co-workers let off a little steam and just have fun. Everyone was usually so polite and professional at the office. Here, she saw them with their families. Sarah kept an eye out for Paul. He and his dogs seemed to be having a great time. He kept grinning and gently teasing all of his employees.

She watched the men and a few women play softball. Paul had tried to get everyone to play, but Sarah and a few of the other women declined. Sarah was wearing a sundress and sandals, not exactly the right gear in which to play softball. So, instead, she and a few of her co-workers watched the game from the sidelines, along with the little kids and the dogs. Mutt and Jeff had claimed her for their own. They were great friends by now, after spending quite a few days together at the Royal Garden. Sarah stroked their smooth heads and silky ears while she watched the softball game.

She tried not to watch Paul too openly, but it was difficult. He was hands down the most attractive man on the field. He was wearing some blue jean cutoffs and a baby blue polo shirt. It made the most of his dark wavy hair, bright blue eyes, and wonderful tan. Sarah did not want the other women to say anything about her interest in Paul, so she yelled compliments for each of the players. They were all showing off for their families and for their co-workers. After the softball game, Paul came over to her to reclaim his dogs. Sarah's eyes were sparkling, and happiness spilled out of her. Paul wanted to stay and talk with her some more but was afraid that his employees might see how attracted he was to her. With a flippant thanks for watching his dogs, he sauntered off with some of the other men. Later that afternoon, Paul came looking for Sarah. He wanted to know what kind of meat she wanted on the grill.

"Well, I do like chicken and shrimp, but my very favorite meat is a great big steak," Sarah said with relish.

Paul felt delighted that she liked steak. It was his favorite meat, as well. "I suppose you like it burnt, don't you?" he teased her.

"No way, I like my steak a nice Medium to Medium-Well," she retorted, with her hands on her hips.

Paul thought that she was just about the cutest thing he ever saw. He was having a very difficult time keeping himself from grabbing her by the hands, running away into a secret place, and kissing the stuffing out of her. Instead, he grinned and turned away, saying over his shoulder, "Well, I hope that there will be one left for you. It seems as if most of the people want their steaks done to Medium, as well."

She ran after him, laughing, and said, "I think I'll come and stand by the grill for a while, just to make sure that you don't give MY steak away."

Paul thought that she was so much fun to be around, especially when she was in a sweet and sassy mood.

The day was a huge success. Towards the end of the day, the gifts were handed out. The employees were touched and delighted by their very generous gifts. When Sarah's turn came, Paul presented her with a huge bouquet of summer flowers, smelling gorgeous.

"For you, my lady," he drawled as he bowed to her. Tucked inside the flowers was a glossy envelope. Inside the envelope, Sarah found a $100 gift certificate for her favorite nursery, *All Things Bright and Beautiful*. There was also a generous gift certificate for her favorite pasta place in town.

"Wow," Sarah breathed. "This is absolutely marvelous. Thank you, everyone." Sarah was so delighted with her gift that she went around and hugged every one of her co-workers. When she came to Paul, she only hesitated for a millisecond before throwing her arms around him and giving him the best hug of his life. Cheeks red, she went back to her chair to watch Paul open his gift. Sarah thought that Paul had a flush on his face. He was probably embarrassed by her hug. If she only knew how he really felt about it, she would have been astonished!

Sarah had prevailed upon the newest employee to present Paul with his gift. They had given him a bronze sculpture of two Labrador dogs, the very image of Mutt and Jeff. At the bottom of the sculpture was a small plaque that said, "Paul Thompson, Boss of the Year" and the date. Paul held it up, looked at his dogs, then looked at his employees, and grinned a huge grin. "This is the best present that I have ever gotten! Thank you all so much. This has been a terrific year for us."

Sarah had asked a local photographer to come to the picnic and take pictures. He got some great candid and action pictures of everyone having a great time. He also had them take a group picture so that each of them could have a memento of their lovely day. The picture turned out extraordinarily well. There were happy faces all around. Later that next week, Paul gave them each their own copy in a beautiful silver frame.

After the very successful annual picnic, Paul felt the urge to get to know his employees better. He remembered the wonderful time that everyone had at the picnic. One day, a few days after the picnic, Paul followed Sarah into the company break room at lunch time. It was pouring with rain outside, so Sarah had decided to eat in, instead of going for her usual walk. There were clusters of his employees sitting around the tables and on the couches and easy chairs. Paul had always prided himself on his comfortable break room. He knew that his employees worked hard and deserved a decent place to eat lunch or take a break from their work. The minute Paul walked into the room all eyes riveted on him. Conversation stopped abruptly. No one had ever seen Paul in the break room before.

He felt a little uncomfortable, but he smiled and said, "This looks like a comfortable place to eat my lunch. Does anyone mind if I have it in here with you?" No one spoke for almost twenty seconds.

Finally, Sarah said, "It would be great if you joined us, Mr. Thompson. Please sit here, with us, if you would like to." Paul looked at the comfortable chair pulled up to a table where four of his employees were sitting.

He smiled and nodded his head. "Yes, thanks, this looks like a comfy spot," he told her.

He walked back to his office and came back with his usual salad and a cold bottle of flavored water. He sat down next to Sarah and started to eat. After a quiet few moments, Sarah struck up a conversation with one of her co-workers. Anna had a new grandson and loved to talk about him to anyone who would listen. Paul listened, without saying anything. After about ten minutes, people started to talk more naturally and even asked Paul a question or two. Paul was pleasant and responded warmly to the people in the break room.

After that first day in the break room, Paul often came into lunch with his employees. They lost their initial shyness with him and started looking forward to his presence at lunch. This is where Paul first talked with Sarah about her beautiful mug. He noticed that she always brought it with her on her breaks. She told him that she loved it because it was so beautiful, even with the small defect on the bottom. That was her philosophy about people, too. She did not expect people to be perfect. She thought people were beautiful even with their warts and all--even more so, with their imperfections. Paul thought that that was an admirable way to think. He wondered, amusingly, what warts she thought he had.

CHAPTER
SEVEN

Sarah had another visit from Ms. Belinda Rhodes. It was getting towards the end of the day. Sarah was walking around the waiting room, picking up things and getting the room ready for the next day. Belinda came in, throwing the door open with a crash.

"Where is Paul?" she demanded in her high, shrill voice. "He is late picking me up. He was supposed to take me to the airport half an hour ago. He knew that I wanted to visit a few shops before my plane came in. Oh, I could just slap him for making me wait," she exclaimed in a tight and angry voice.

Sarah calmly looked at Belinda and said, "Mr. Thompson is in a meeting right now with someone from the county office. The meeting was delayed because the officer had some emergency before he could get here. It is a really important meeting regarding some big project that they will be working on next week."

Belinda made a rude noise and said, "Well, I don't care if he is meeting with the President of the United States. He needs to take me to the airport."

Sarah looked at her watch and asked Belinda, "What time does your flight leave, Ms. Rhodes?"

Belinda looked at her defiantly and said, "It doesn't matter what time it leaves. Paul said he would drive me, and so he needs to drive me."

Sarah, who saw that Belinda would not be appeased, reluctantly went to knock on Paul's office door.

There was a short silence in the murmur from the other side of the door, and then his voice saying testily, "Come in." He looked up, frowning, at Sarah standing in the doorway.

Sarah said hurriedly, "I'm sorry sir, but Ms. Rhodes is here and very upset. She insists that I tell you that she is waiting for her ride to the airport. What do you want me to do?"

Paul, still frowning, looked at his guest in the office. "I can't leave right now. Please tell Ms. Rhodes that I have been delayed. Either put her into a taxi or take her to the airport yourself, Miss Brewster. I will make sure that you are reimbursed for your time and the trip. Now please let me get back to my meeting. Good night, Miss Brewster," he said with a snap. Sarah backed out of the room, quite taken aback. Paul was usually not so abrupt with her.

She looked at Belinda and said in a calm voice that concealed her indignant feelings, "Ms. Rhodes, Mr. Thompson suggests that you either take a taxi to the airport or let me drive you there. What would you prefer?"

Belinda said huffily, "Well, I suppose you would be better than another taxi. Get my luggage from that taxi waiting outside. Oh, and pay him off for me, I don't have any smaller bills on me. Look sharp, Miss. I'm already late."

Sarah fumed and got her purse from her desk. "I'm ready now, Ms. Rhodes. Please follow me out to my car. I'll pick up your luggage on my way," Sarah spoke in a dangerously quiet voice. Anyone who knew her well would have known that Sarah was in one of her very rare tempers. Ms. Rhodes, who didn't care about anyone's feelings but her own, was oblivious. She followed Sarah out to the taxi. Sarah spoke pleasantly, but through clenched teeth, to the driver. Since Ms. Rhodes had so much luggage, he would not allow Sarah to take it out and carry it all the way to the parking lot, where her car was parked. He told her to bring her car next to his cab and he would off-load it for her. Belinda waited next to the cab while Sarah went to get her car. Sarah was seething but trying to maintain a professional demeanor. The driver loaded all of Belinda's luggage into Sarah's trunk. Sarah paid him, giving him a generous tip. Paul had said that he would reimburse her, and in her anger at him, she made sure that he would have to repay her hefty tip. Sarah made small talk with Belinda as she drove to the airport. She wondered how Paul could stand Belinda. She was the most egocentric person that Sarah had ever met. Belinda cared nothing for anyone but herself. Once at the airport, Sarah got a porter to take all of Belinda's luggage.

Belinda nodded at Sarah and said, "Well, at least you seem to have some common sense. Tell Paul that I will call him this weekend. I will expect him to pick me up when I fly back in on Sunday." With that, she turned on her heels and followed the porter into the airport.

"Well," thought Sarah with a grimace. "She didn't even thank me for the ride. Good riddance to her," Sarah said out loud. She drove home, thinking about Paul and Belinda. She should back off from the sweet friendship that had formed between Paul and herself. She did not want to get in the way of Paul and Belinda's relationship. She thought that Paul was really getting to like her, though. She loved him, but he had already given his pledge to

Ms. Rhodes. How very sorry she was for him. If Paul did indeed marry Belinda, he would have to put up with her selfishness for the rest of his life. She was sad, just thinking about it. She looked around her pretty apartment and felt better. She put on her favorite guitar instrumental music and curled up on the couch with a good book. That would soon soothe her back into a more mellow frame of mind.

Paul finished his meeting with the county officer. He felt bad about the snappy way he had spoken to Sarah. He didn't know what they had decided to do; had Sarah put Belinda into a taxi, or had she driven Belinda to the airport? He still had so much work to do before his meetings next week. He would have to work the whole weekend. It would be so much better if he could get Sarah to help him with the work. She could type while he dictated his letters to her. She could help him make up the spreadsheets and other documents that he needed for the meetings. Of course, after the way he treated her before she left, she would probably not want to help him in the least little bit. He hated it when his temper got the better of him. He tried hard to always be calm and professional at the office. Belinda had been at her most annoying, as well. Somehow, he was going to have to get Sarah to forgive him for his behavior and then ask her to help him out this weekend. He knew that Sarah was the most amenable of girls. Her gentle friendliness and professional demeanor were legendary at work. He usually tried to keep his weekends free so that he could see his family and relax from the pressures of work, but he had just plain run out of time on that Friday. He nervously raked his hand through his hair. He would have to call her at home. The phone rang at Sarah's house, just as she was fixing her supper.

"Hello, Sarah. Am I interrupting anything?" Paul asked in a hesitantly friendly voice.

Sarah, who had not quite mellowed out since she had gotten home, said coolly, "Hello. No, I'm just fixing my supper. How can I help you?"

Paul heard the coolness in her voice and winced a little. She was still upset with him. "Well, do you have any plans for this weekend, Sarah?" he asked her in a persistently friendly voice. Her heart started pounding, wondering why he wanted to know.

"Yes, I am dogsitting for Rip this weekend. Clara is going to her niece's wedding out of town. I'm staying the weekend at Clara's house. I can't bring Rip to my apartment because pets are not allowed here. Why do you ask?" she said to him.

"Oh, shoot, I was going to beg you to help me get ready for those two big meetings that I have coming up next week. I know that I can't expect you to work on your days off, but I am really in need of your help if I am going to be ready for the meetings," he said with a grimace.

Sarah knew how important those meetings were to him, and she wanted to help him. She said quietly, "Maybe you could come over to Clara's house, and we could work there. I don't want to leave Rip alone all day."

Paul considered her proposal and then asked, "Do you think that Rip would mind coming to my place? He already knows Mutt and Jeff. They have always gotten along well at the Royal Garden. It's just that I have all of the work at my house, along with the fax machine and copy machine. I couldn't bring everything over to Clara's house. What do you think? Would you be willing to bring Rip along and work at my house? I would like to start working tomorrow morning after breakfast. What do you say, Sarah?"

Sarah considered it for a few moments and then quietly agreed. She planned to go to Clara's house later that evening to settle in.

She and Clara needed to talk about Rip. Clara was planning to get a ride in the morning at 8:00, so Sarah could be free to go to Paul's house any time after that. She told Paul that she could be there by 9:00 am with Rip. He reminded her of the directions to his house.

"Thank you so very much, Sarah. I promise that I will make the time up to you. Or, if you would rather, I can just pay you for the overtime hours. Think about it, and let me know, okay? Oh, and I also want to talk with you about your help with Belinda this afternoon. We can take care of everything tomorrow," he said, with a smile in his voice. Sarah didn't sound too upset anymore, he thought, with satisfaction. He never wanted to upset her, ever again.

Sarah agreed and said good night. She finished her supper and grabbed her overnight bag. She added an extra outfit to the bag. She had planned a very casual weekend with Rip. Now, she would need something a little nicer to wear at Paul's house.

Sarah arrived at Clara's house around 8:30 pm. The evening was still lovely and warm. The two friends sat outside on the deck talking for an hour or so. Rip ran around in the enclosed back yard, making them laugh at his exuberance. Sarah told Clara about Paul's request that she and Rip spend the day at his house. Clara had no issues with that. She knew that Sarah wanted to be helpful to her boss. She also knew that Paul Thompson was engaged to a haughty young woman. He was a perfect gentleman, but she had also seen the way he watched Sarah when they met up at the Royal Gardens. He had feelings for Sarah, she just knew it. However, she was not worried or nervous for Sarah. She knew that Paul would never do anything to hurt her.

The next morning was a mad rush to get Clara away on time. Clara kissed Rip's furry little face before she left. "Be good for Sarah, Rip. I'm going to miss you, you little rascal," Clara said with a smile.

When she arrived at Paul's house and saw him, Sarah was glad that she had worn the pretty green sundress. It looked just right with his casual outfit. He was wearing some khaki shorts and a beautiful blue pullover shirt, the exact color of his eyes. Her normal professional outfit would have stuck out like a sore thumb. Paul led her into his home office. It looked like her office at work. He had all of the computers and other office equipment that she would ever need.

He sat her down on the comfortable chair behind the enormous desk, took Rip from her, and said, "I'll just take this little guy and let him romp around with my two. Don't worry, they won't go anywhere. I have a very large enclosed garden. They should be okay for a few hours while we get some work done."

Paul came back in and looked at Sarah. She looked calm, cool, and pretty. "It is so good of you to come and help me today. I think that I will have you sit in front of the computer so you can type while I dictate to you. I'll sit over here by this table, and that way I can spread out all of the papers and documents that I will need. Are you ready? Can I get you a cold drink before we start?" he asked. Sarah said no and that she was ready to start.

They worked for a good three hours; then they got up and went into the kitchen. Sarah was impressed by all of the modern gadgets she saw in that old-fashioned kitchen. Paul saw her surprised look and interpreted her look correctly.

"Mrs. Kennedy, my wonderful housekeeper, likes her little conveniences. She is a marvelous cook, and I would be lost without her. I try to make her job as easy as I can. I look after her because she looks after me so well. She has been with me for more than ten years," he stated.

He opened the fridge and looked inside. "She has left everything needed for a picnic lunch. I'm starving. I hope you are, too," Paul said with a smile.

Sarah nodded. "How can I help?" she asked him.

"I'll get this food out if you go into those drawers there and get some silverware. Also, the glasses and plates are in that cupboard over there," he pointed.

They took everything outside to the deck and sat at the pretty white wrought iron table that overlooked his large garden. They watched the dogs romp around and talked casually about the work they had just finished and what still needed to be done that afternoon. When they finished eating, Paul whistled for the dogs and fed and watered them. The three dogs ran over to a shady spot in the garden and lay down to have a nap. They had played around all morning and were tuckered out. After Paul came back onto the deck, Sarah helped him carry everything back into the house. Paul refused to let her help clean up. He told her to go and explore his garden.

Sarah walked around the garden. It was lovely. It looked like it had been planned by a professional. There was a vegetable garden bordered by fruit trees at the rear of the garden. One whole side was taken up with a wildflower garden. Near the deck was a more formal garden, planted with a bright profusion of fragrant flowers. As Sarah walked around on the paths, she named all of the flowers in her head. How her father would have loved to see this beautiful place, she thought. The entire garden was surrounded by a stone wall. The wall looked old and a bit crumbly, but it was so charming. There were a few rustic tables and chairs and benches placed strategically around the garden. This was a place where someone could sit and pleasantly dream away hours of time, she thought. Sarah always thought that you could tell a lot about a person from their garden. This garden was telling her that Paul loved this outdoor space. The vegetable garden was probably where he got all of his vegetables for the salads that he ate for lunch every day at the office. The wildflower garden was colorful and made Sarah just want to sit down right in the middle of it all, or maybe lay down in it. The sun was shining, and the breeze was warm, without being too hot. If she had been alone, Sarah might have done just that. But this was Paul's garden, and they had work to finish. She sighed and went to sit on the bench next to the formal garden.

Paul came out a few minutes later. "Like it?" he asked, with a note of happiness in his voice.

"Oh, yes," she replied. "This is a really lovely garden. I envy you, getting to look at it and spending your free time here every day," she said wistfully.

He looked at her and thought how very right she looked, sitting in his garden, with the sun shining on her pretty hair. The wind was blowing a little and her hair, loose and shiny, blew around her face. She lifted her hand to capture a handful of it. She sat there, holding onto her hair, eyes closed, face lifted to the sun, just breathing deeply of the warm fragrant flowers. Paul wanted to kiss her more than he had ever wanted to kiss anyone in his life. She was so perfect, so lovely, so right for him.

He turned his head away from her and said, "Come on Sarah, we have that work to finish. If we get done by suppertime, I will take you out to eat. You can choose wherever you would like to go. Are you ready?"

Sarah reluctantly opened her eyes, smiled at him, and got up to go into the house. She found her purse and grabbed a scrunchy from it and then followed him back into his office. She used the scrunchy to put her messy hair into a loosely gathered ponytail. Paul saw that with regret. He loved her hair, especially when it was a little messy. He could picture her, resting her head against his shoulders while he lightly stroked her hair. It looked so soft and silky. He went back to his table, put her out of his thoughts with a herculean effort, and got back to work. Sarah sat back down at the computer and waited for further instructions. They worked for five more hours, finishing everything just as the grandfather clock in the hall chimed 7:00 pm.

Paul straightened up, stretched his back, and said, "There, that should do it. I think that we have done everything that we can to be ready for those meetings next week. I could never have done it without you, Sarah. You get to pick where you want to go out for supper." He looked at her with a warm smile.

Sarah closed down the computer and stood up and stretched, as well. "What about the dogs?" she asked him.

"We'll feed them before we go out," Paul said.

"I'm not dressed to go anywhere fancy," she told him. "Can we just go and get a burger or something? I would love to go back into your garden after supper. I just love sitting in a garden when the sun starts to go down, and the fireflies come out," she said with a shy smile.

"Great, why don't I run and get some burgers and fries while you walk with the dogs. I won't be very long. What kind of burger do you like?" he asked her. She told him her preferences and watched him leave.

Sarah went into the garden and played with the dogs. Paul got back about half an hour later, laden down with burgers, fries, onion rings, bowls of fruit and salad, and little apple pies.

"Wow, when you go out to pick up supper, you really get into it," she exclaimed, laughing.

He shrugged and grinned and said, "I owe you so much. The least I can do is feed you right."

"Well, there will probably be enough left for you to have for lunch, tomorrow," she retorted, laughingly.

"Oh no, I am pretty hungry. I bet we can make a serious dent in this pile of food," he said, hungrily.

They laughed and talked while they ate their food, sitting comfortably at the table on the deck. The sun went down while they sat there, talking about everything under the sun. Paul could not remember the last time that he had enjoyed himself so much. The night air was silky and magical. He could have had the night go on forever. Sarah felt the same way. She looked at her watch and found that it was after 10:00 pm. She regretfully said that she and Rip should get going. Paul did not want her to leave, and he reluctantly stood up and helped take in all of the food containers to the kitchen. She went to get her purse while Paul rounded up Rip. He walked them to her car and gently set Rip on her back seat. He came around to Sarah's door and took her hands in his.

"Thank you, again, Sarah. You have been such a great help to me. This was an amazing day. I won't forget this. Make sure and let me know how you want to be repaid for your hours today." He looked at her and was reminded about yesterday at the office. "Oh, by the way, what did you do about Belinda yesterday? Did you put her in a taxi, or did you drive her to the airport? Whatever you did, please let me reimburse you for it," he said, still holding her hands.

Sarah stiffened in resentment. She had just had a perfectly lovely day and had been thinking of Paul in all kinds of romantic ways. Now she came back to earth with a thump. Of course, Paul was just grateful for her help. This day had been one of the best days of her life because she had spent it with Paul, helping him with his work. They had talked like they were real friends. Now Paul had spoiled her day by reminding her that he expected to pay her for her help. She would have gladly helped him for free.

She gently took back her hands and said in a chilly voice, "I gave Ms. Rhodes a ride to the airport and paid off her taxi, which she had taken to come to the office. I'll give you the bill on Monday, okay, Mr. Thompson?"

Paul looked surprised and upset and said a little angrily, "Mr. Thompson? I thought that I was Paul. Why did you say that Sarah?"

She looked down at her hands so he could not see the tears that had started to form in her eyes. "Well, you keep reminding me that you want to pay me. I feel like I was at work all day. I call you Mr. Thompson at work, don't I?" she responded, huffily.

Paul looked at her tenderly. "Oh, Sarah, you silly goose. I just meant that I did not expect you to do all of that work for nothing. I didn't mean to hurt your feelings. I would never, knowingly, hurt you. Don't you know that by now?" he asked her softly.

She looked up at him, her green eyes still glistening with unshed tears. Paul said something muffled under his breath and pulled her into his arms for a tight hug. "I'm sorry, Sarah. Please don't feel hurt. I won't say anything more about it. Just don't feel bad anymore, okay?" he pleaded softly.

She nodded and closed her eyes for a second, savoring the feel of his arms around her. "I'm sorry that I was so silly, Paul," she said as she gently pulled away from him. "I'm okay. I should go home now."

Paul nodded and let her go. As she got into her car, he told her to drive carefully. She had told him that it had only taken her about twenty minutes to drive from Clara's house to his. He looked in his address book, where she had written Clara's name and phone number. Half an hour after she left, he called Clara's house. Sarah answered the phone right away.

"Hi, Sarah. I just wanted to make sure that you got back to Clara's house safely. Are you going to the Royal Garden tomorrow afternoon?" Paul asked.

Sarah was surprised, but touched, that Paul had called to make sure that she was safely home. She felt that she needed a little break from Paul, though. She needed time to get her feelings back under control by Monday. She responded calmly, "Thank you, Paul, for checking up on me. Rip and I are fine. Actually, I have other plans for us tomorrow. I'm sorry. I heard that it was supposed to rain tomorrow. I don't like to take Rip out in the rain. He goes a little crazy in the mud." Paul did not say anything, so she added, "Do Mutt and Jeff like walking in the rain?"

"Oh yes, we all like walking in the rain. Okay, have fun tomorrow. I'll see you on Monday," Paul said, a little coolly.

"Good night, Paul. See you on Monday," Sarah responded back at him. They both hung up the phones, dissatisfied with the way their lovely day had ended.

Paul was disappointed because he would have loved to spend another day, or part of a day, in Sarah's company. They fit together so well. He wondered if Sarah could tell how he felt about her. Knowing Sarah, she was making it easy for him to remember that he was an engaged man. Come to think of it, he should remember it, too. It was just so hard to get into the right frame of mind to spend time with Belinda when he would much rather be with Sarah. Belinda would have hated today. She got angry when he had to work on the weekends. She would have insisted that he take her out to some popular place to eat. Forget walking the dogs or having a picnic lunch or even sitting on the deck just talking and enjoying the beautiful weather and the garden.

Paul savored his lovely day with Sarah while he took the dogs for one last long walk. He went to bed that night, remembering that he would have to pick up Belinda at the airport tomorrow. He hoped that she would be too tired from her trip to want to talk much or go out. But somehow, he doubted that. She would expect to be wined and dined at the most popular restaurant in town. He was profoundly glad that he and Sarah had finished his work today. He felt sure that his Sunday would be fully taken up, keeping Belinda entertained.

CHAPTER

EIGHT

Sarah continued to do her wonderful best at work. She stayed professional and politely friendly with Paul. She went out on a few dates with a new guy, who was a friend of Susan's. They had double-dated once or twice. She was doing her best to get on with her life, without seeing too much of Paul. She felt a deep ache in her heart every day when she saw him and spent time with him, taking down his letters and listening to his instructions for the day. He was spending more and more time with his other employees at the office. He was often out of his office, sitting in the waiting room, talking with his staff. The rest of the summer and early autumn was very pleasant at the workplace. The employees were happy and felt kindly towards Paul and each other. The workload increased a bit and people were busy, but they liked their jobs even more than ever before.

It seemed like the more Sarah tried to distance herself from Paul, the more he was around. She had stopped going to the Royal Garden every Sunday. Paul still went there often, wondering where Sarah was. He wanted to find out what was going on with her. He spent hours out of his office, talking with his other employees, just to catch a few more glimpses of Sarah, sitting at her desk and working. She was as sweet and friendly as ever, but he felt the barrier that she had erected between them.

He knew by now that he was head over heels in love with her. He definitely had to do something about Belinda. Now was the time. Belinda had been out of town for three weeks or so, visiting friends in Illinois. She was due back in Litton on the weekend. He started to make a plan to go and see her. He would gauge her feelings for him and about marriage in general. He hated to hurt her, but he could no longer be her fiancé, knowing that he loved Sarah. He dreamed about the day when he could ask Sarah out on a date. He hoped that she liked him a lot, or even, he hoped in his innermost heart, that she secretly loved him, as he loved her.

He knew that he did not want to date Sarah while she was his secretary. He would have to see about hiring a new secretary. He would have to do that without Sarah's knowledge, though. After he asked her out, and they went on their first date, he would know better about her feelings for him. If she loved him, he wanted to ask her to marry him, have the world's quickest engagement, and get married as soon as she agreed to it. He knew that he was getting ahead of himself, but he just could not stop his eager planning. He had a week-long trip to Los Angeles coming up. He would get his plans made before it, end his relationship with Belinda, and then embark on the most exciting and promising time of his life. His life, with Sarah at his side.

That weekend, Paul called Belinda, who had just arrived home from her visit to her friends in Illinois. He asked if he could come over to see her. He thought that she sounded reluctant to meet up with him, but she told him that she wanted a meal out at their favorite steak house. He agreed to pick her up at 7:00 pm. He did not plan to tell her about Sarah. He just wanted to find out about Belinda's feelings about himself and about their engagement.

He got to her house a little ahead of time. She was not ready for him. After waiting for more than an hour for her to be ready, Paul was getting annoyed. He sat, barely talking to her mother, while he waited. When Belinda came into the room with a flourish, he looked at her. She was wearing some outrageous outfit. It was leather and lace, trailing in some places, and very tight in other places. It made her look like a tall exotic bird. He hid his amused thoughts and bent forward to kiss her cheek.

She said, "Darling, don't mess up my hair. I wanted to look wonderful for you, tonight. I just bought this new dress. Isn't it gorgeous?"

He smiled kindly and said, "It's out of this world. You look very well. Obviously, your vacation agreed with you."

She preened and said, "Yes, I know. I'm ready. Let's go."

They went to a well-known steak house. Everyone who wanted to be noticed was there. Paul liked it for the great steaks, while Belinda liked it for its well-known reputation of having the most prominent people in town as regular patrons. She did not like steak. She preferred shrimp or lobster and a salad. They were seated at a good table, overlooking the scenic backyard. Paul and Belinda nodded hello to several people they knew while they perused the menu.

After Paul asked her what she wanted and ordered for them, he sat back and really looked at Belinda. She was an attractive woman in her early thirties, who spent hours every day trying to hold onto her good looks. She didn't have any type of job or do any good work for charities. She spent all day, every day, doing things to please herself. He thought back to when they had gotten engaged more than two years ago.

He couldn't believe that he had fallen for her charade about how she loved children and admired him for all of the work he did with the local youth clubs. He had thought that she would fit into his life so well. He had been attracted to her, even a little in love with her. She had eagerly accepted his proposal of marriage. Paul's business was thriving at that time. He was starting to make a name for himself in the business world. It had seemed like a good idea, at the time, to get engaged. Soon after they had gotten engaged Belinda told him that she was not in a hurry to get married. She enjoyed having a handsome and well-connected escort for all of the parties and events that she liked to go to.

That had been fine with Paul for about a year. After a while, he started to realize that they wanted vastly different things. He enjoyed going out in the evenings and meeting people and expanding his company. But more than that, he was essentially a home-loving man, who enjoyed walking with his dogs, eating a good supper that his excellent housekeeper came up with night after night, and spending quality time with a woman who shared his interests and visions. He knew now that that woman was not Belinda. It was Sarah. How he longed to have Sarah sitting together with him--all snuggled up on the couch, listening to music and talking or just being quiet, but being at peace together. Belinda loved the nightlife. She was bored sitting at home. She hated dogs. Even if he hurt her, he knew that now was the time to end their engagement.

After sitting in the restaurant for over two hours, socializing with people he barely knew, Paul was ready to go home. Belinda wanted to stay and talk with her acquaintances for a while longer. She longed to be seen by more people. She glared at Paul when he suggested, for the third time, that they should get going. He wanted to talk with her, and they certainly could not have a private conversation when people kept dropping by their table every few minutes.

Belinda was certainly not in the mood to listen to anything serious. She pouted for about fifteen minutes until Paul finally dipped into his pocket and withdrew his billfold. He quietly told her that he would pay for her taxi home if she felt the need to stay. Belinda knew that she was not going to get her way, so she reluctantly allowed him to usher her out to his car. Once in the car, she turned towards him and started complaining bitterly about his treatment of her.

Paul listened courteously, pursing his lips together, so as not to say the things he longed to say to her. He waited a long time for her to stop complaining. Then he took her hand and said that they needed to talk. He said that he had waited for over two years for them to get married. He wanted them to either get married or break their engagement. She looked shocked and started to protest. She told him that she was having too much fun to get married. Why couldn't they just stay engaged for a while longer? Belinda liked her lifestyle the way it was. She was a free agent, doing whatever she wanted when she wanted to do it. She enjoyed having a handsome fiance to take her out. She knew that her friends were envious of her engagement to one of the town's most eligible bachelors. She knew that if they married, she would have to give up some of the things that she was used to doing. Besides, she liked to flirt with handsome men. She thought about that extremely attractive man that she had met a few weeks ago when she was visiting her friend in Illinois. She had forbidden her friend to talk about her engagement to Paul. Belinda, herself, said nothing to him about Paul. They had gone to a few parties together, and Belinda had very much enjoyed his company. He had insisted that she take his number with her and to let him look her up if he was ever in her town. Belinda did not even feel guilty about keeping that little secret from Paul. What he did not know would not hurt him.

"Darling, why do we have to decide anything right now?" she demanded in her shrill voice. He looked at her quietly and told her that the time had come to make up her mind about what she wanted to do, get married or call off their engagement. She wasn't prepared to give him her final decision at that moment, so she begged for a little more time. He told her about his trip to Los Angeles in a week. He said that he would give her two weeks to decide, but he would expect her answer when he returned from Los Angeles on that Sunday evening. Belinda agreed to that. She turned her head away and would not even let him kiss her on the cheek when she got out of the car.

Paul turned his car for home. He was pretty sure that Belinda did not love him or want to marry him anymore. He had tried to call her bluff by insisting they get married now or break off their engagement. What if he was wrong? What if she agreed to marry him right away? He did not want that. He did not plan to marry her. What if he just made his situation worse? He would have to wait until he came back from Los Angeles to find out what she wanted to do. He hoped with all his heart that she would want to break their engagement. He knew that if she did not break it, he would have to do it. What a mess!!

The next week, Paul thought about his troubles with Belinda. He met some possible secretarial candidates at his home because he did not want Sarah to even catch a whiff of anything having to do with a secretary who would replace her. He found a replacement for Sarah who he really enjoyed meeting. He had never had a male secretary before, but this young man, Jim Bacon, seemed to be a good fit for Paul's company. He hired Jim and told him that he would be starting on October 10th.

Of course, if Sarah did not love him or want to marry him, he would help her get another job. He knew a few other businessmen who would love to have someone like Sarah working for them. She would not be stuck without a job because he had hired Jim. If, after he broke his engagement with Belinda and asked Sarah out, she was not interested in having a relationship with him, Paul would feel so uncomfortable, that he didn't think he would be able to see her in his office every day. She might be upset with him, as well, and he bet that she would not want to stay in his employ after that. He was taking such a big risk in hiring Jim, but he knew that once he was free from Belinda, he would not be able to stop himself from wanting to start a relationship with Sarah. It was a mess, he thought gloomily.

Paul was distracted at the office and not his usual calm and friendly self. His employees wondered what was going on with him. Sarah was extra kind and considerate regarding her interactions with Paul. She thought that he was worried about the upcoming trip to Los Angeles, for some reason. She would have to wait and find out. Things would be back to normal after he came back from his trip.

That Sunday afternoon, Sarah went to visit Ben and Josie. Their garden was lovely, a deliciously scented bright and beautiful place. They were in the garden when she got there. They had a picnic supper in the garden, sitting at the rustic little table set amidst the blooms. The weather was just right, bright blue skies with a warm fragrant breeze. They talked and laughed for several hours before Sarah finally got up to go home. Ben hugged Sarah and told her to take some flowers with her. Josie had cut some of Sarah's favorites as they were chatting. After a long hug with Josie, Sarah reluctantly turned to leave. She just loved these two longtime warm-hearted friends. As she drove home, she chuckled when she remembered the hilarious story that Ben had told them about an absolutely horrible customer that he had that afternoon. It seems that a young woman named Ms. Rhodes had come into the nursery to pick up flowers for a special dinner party that she would be attending. Ben had been fertilizing some flower beds outside. His boss was busy, so he called Ben into the building

94

to wait on Ms. Rhodes. Ben had not had time to wash his hands before he greeted her. Her shrill, demanding voice brought up a defensive mood in Ben. She was condescending to him and looked down her nose at him. "Something smells in here!" she said disdainfully.

Ben tried not to grin and said, "No ma'am, it's just things growing as they ought to be. How can I help you?" Ben was good at his job and knew his flowers well. He suggested some likely flowers for the large bouquet that she wanted to take to the party. While he was gathering them, he kept inwardly cringing at her shrill voice. At last, she was satisfied with the variety of flowers for the bouquet. Ben lovingly wrapped up the beautiful and fragrant bunch and handed the parcel to her. His unwashed hand had left a very slight smear of manure on the white package. Ms. Rhodes shrieked loudly and dropped the bundle onto the ground.

She said loudly, "Look at that! I can't take these flowers. This is disgusting. You should be fired for this!"

Ben's boss came running when he heard her shrill screaming voice. She pointed to the parcel with the very slight smear on it and demanded new flowers. She wanted Ben to be fired and she kept on complaining for a good five minutes. The boss nodded at Ben to go. Ben left them to go and wash his hands. He stayed away for a while longer, giving his boss a chance to take care of the situation. When he came back, the boss was shaking his head and muttering under his breath. Ben approached him warily, not knowing what his boss would say. He was so very relieved when his boss looked at Ben and burst out laughing. He had given her a new batch of flowers, telling her that he was going to give her a huge discount for her troubles. Ms. Rhodes had smirked with a pleased look about that and had gladly paid the amount that he asked for.

"I charged her ten dollars more than the original amount, just to make up for the waste of the first flowers," he chortled with glee. They laughed together about it. The boss handed Ben the original bunch of flowers and told him to bring them home for Josie.

"I'm sure that Josie will not reject them, just because of that little smear," he said with a huge grin. Ben apologized for the smear, but his boss said that he understood about it. He had, after all, directed Ben to wait on her without giving him a chance to wash his hands. "Anyone who comes to a nursery should not be too worried about a little bit of fertilizer," he said.

Ben handed the bunch of flowers to Josie when he got home. They had a really good laugh about it. While Sarah was driving home, she thought about the story. Somehow she just knew that 'Ms. Rhodes' was Paul's fiancee.

That Monday afternoon in late September, the day before Paul was to leave for his Los Angeles trip, Sarah knocked on Paul's door just before she left for the day. When she did not get an answer, she quietly walked into the room. Paul was still sitting at his desk staring at the wall. She was concerned to see his gray and weary face. Sarah asked him if he felt all right. Paul shook his head but looked up at her as she leaned over his desk. His face was bleak and the words, when they came out, were soft but barely controlled.

"My life is such a mess! I have been a fool, and I don't know what I am going to do about it."

Sarah's soft heart ached for him and his pain. "It will be okay," she said softly. She gently put her hand on his arm and patted it.

He looked up, saw her compassion, and quickly got up and moved around the side of his desk. He caught her hands in his, drawing her close to him. His arms closed gently around her and he bent his head to kiss her mouth. His mouth was hard and demanding at first but quickly gentled into a soft and tender kiss.

He broke away, shocked, and said, "Oh, I do beg your pardon! I should never have done that! Please go home now. I will lock everything up. Remember that I will be in Los Angeles for a week. I will be back in the office next Monday. You have my cell phone number in case you need to get a hold of me urgently." Sarah nodded and left the office without saying anything else to him. She felt shaken by the power of his kiss.

As she walked out of his office, Sarah was struck again by the overwhelming feeling of love that she felt for Paul. Why did she have to do something so stupid as to fall in love with an engaged man? She had to be so careful that he did not see how she felt about him. It was something she would have to keep hidden for as long as she worked for him. She felt very sad that Paul was hurting. She wondered if he was starting to fall in love with her, knowing that he was already engaged to Belinda. She hoped so with all of her heart, although having met Belinda on several occasions, she knew that Belinda was not likely to give him up. Belinda was willful and selfish. Sarah doubted that Belinda even loved Paul, but he was handsome and wealthy, and she knew a good thing when she had it. Sarah could try and lure Paul away from Belinda, but she knew she wouldn't do that. She was a kind and fair young woman, and she would never be happy with herself if she did that. Paul must have loved Belinda at one time to have asked her to be his wife. Sarah decided that the only thing she could do was to start looking for another job and remove herself. Paul would forget her in time and marry Belinda.

The next day, Sarah was surprised to have a visitor. He was a slight young man with a pronounced limp.

He smiled at Sarah and said, "Hello, my name is Jim Bacon. Mr. Thompson hired me to take over the job of secretary from someone named Sarah Brewster. I know that I'm not supposed to start until October 10th, but I wondered if anyone could show me around. I came to the city to see my girlfriend, Betty, but she was busy. I thought that I would get some information about the job while I had some free time. I want to drive around and look at apartments, too. We'll be getting married in a month or so, and I want to surprise her with some housing options."

Sarah was so shocked and surprised that she couldn't say anything for a minute or two. Jim asked to sit down because his leg was aching. Sarah sat him down in the chair in front of her desk and looked down at her feet, trying to get her feelings under control.

A few seconds later she said, "I'm Sarah Brewster. Nice to meet you, Mr. Bacon."

Jim smiled at her and asked, "Are you leaving to get married, Miss Brewster?"

"No, no, I'm taking another job. This is a nice place to work, though. I'm sure you will like Mr. Thompson and all of the rest of the staff very much," Sarah tried to say it all calmly, even though she was dying a little inside. So, Paul was going to fire her, was he? What about her two weeks' notice? Sarah recovered her calm and started asking him more questions.

Jim stated that he was recovering from a car accident. He planned to get married to his girl as soon as he could find a home for them to live in. Betty currently lived with her mother but was not happy there. He had extensive experience as a secretary, having worked for a large agricultural firm. He wanted to move away from the small town he had grown up in and worked in. Betty liked a bigger town and all of the theaters and shopping available there. They talked for an hour or so about the job.

Sarah told her co-workers that she would answer the telephone when it rang. Her voice was nicely under control when Paul called later that afternoon to check in. She was able to say that everything was running smoothly and that there were no pressing calls for him to return. Paul hung up, thinking that Sarah had sounded abrupt. He decided to call again each day just to make sure that everything was fine. He hated to be away from her for so long, but he had no choice but to be in Los Angeles for his business. He couldn't wait to come back home and go into his office to see Sarah again. But he would see Belinda first and break off their engagement, even if she did not want it to end. Now was his and Sarah's time to be happy.

Sarah invited Jim to come back to the office for a few hours the next day, as well. She wanted to show him some of the projects that she was now working on. She found out that Jim had a quick mind and was very creative. He would be a great secretary for Paul. Sarah decided that she really liked him and could have become friends with him in different circumstances.

She now desperately needed to look for another job and leave before Paul came back on Monday. She was so unhappy and upset that he wanted her gone. He had not even whispered that he found her to be unsatisfactory on the job. Maybe he needed to get her out of the office because he was starting to really like her, and that would never do because of Belinda. Either way, she planned to leave without a trace. She looked in a large variety of papers to see if she could find a new job that was miles away. She would have to give up her apartment, too.

On Thursday morning, Sarah finally found a job. *"Wanted: experienced secretary. Free housing in the annex next to a large mine in Brazil. Fabulous wages. Must have no dependents and must sign a three-month contract."* There was a phone number to call. She called it and had a phone interview. She faxed over three references and was called back that same day. They wanted her to come at once. She made plans to leave the United States on Sunday evening. Now she had to pack up her belongings, rent out her home, sell her car, and leave. If she couldn't find someone to sublet her apartment, she would have to keep it and pay the rent while she was gone. She hoped it would not come to that. She knew quite a few young people through her church that she could ask. Then she remembered that Jim Bacon had said that he was looking for an apartment close to work. Sarah called Jim at the number that he had left. He and Betty agreed to come into the office and talk with her on Friday afternoon.

Sarah let herself into the office very early on Friday morning. She cleaned out her desk and walked around looking at everything one last time. Since she had forgotten to bring in her company picnic picture, she went into Paul's office and took down his copy from the shelf where it had the pride of the place. Everyone was smiling, and they looked like a happy bunch. She took the picture out of the frame and went to Xerox it. It was a good thing that she had just replaced the colored ink. The colors would be crisp and sharp. She enlarged the picture to get just Paul in it. It took several tries to get a very nice and clear copy of him. He looked wonderful, all tanned and happy. His blue shirt made his eyes look amazing. The sun shone on his dark hair and the breeze had blown it all around. He looked successful, confident, and very handsome. She put the original photo back into its frame and put it back on the shelf.

Sarah lovingly gazed at his face and then put it in the small box with her other belongings. She took the box out to her car and locked it in her trunk before the rest of the staff came in to work. No one had asked her who Jim Bacon was, and she did not offer any information, either. No one at the office knew anything about her plan to leave that day. She didn't want them to have to keep any information from Paul, in case he asked them about her departure. She felt sad that she couldn't say goodbye to them. She had become quite friendly with all of them in the seven months that she had worked there.

Sarah wanted to leave some kind of note for Paul but had a really difficult time writing it. The lump in her throat threatened to choke her. Crying a little, she sat down at his desk, running her hand along the smooth wood and gazing around at the pictures of him and his family on the shelves. In the end, she took one of his plain note cards from his desk and simply wrote, "Goodbye Paul. Have a happy life." -- Sarah

She sealed the card in an envelope, wrote his name on the front, and left it on his desk where he could find it right away when he came in on Monday.

Sarah got through the day somehow. She felt near to tears all day, but she presented her usual calm and friendly front to her co-workers and any visitors. She geared herself up to taking Paul's phone call that afternoon. When the phone rang at 3:30 pm, she just knew that it was Paul. He had called every day that week at that approximate time.

"Hello, this is Miss Brewster speaking," Sarah said in her quiet pleasant voice.

"Sarah, I only have a few minutes before I have to go into another meeting. Is there anything that I need to know about before I get back on Monday?" Paul asked her in a hurried voice.

"No, Mr. Thompson, there is nothing that you need to know about until Monday. I won't keep you because I know you're busy. Have a nice flight back," she said quietly, careful to keep her voice friendly. Paul hung up the phone and hurried to his meeting. Sarah teared up, thinking that this was the last time she would ever hear his beloved voice again. Her last words to him had been, "Have a nice flight back." How surprised he would be when he came into the office on Monday and found Jim Bacon sitting at her desk, she thought. While she was still upset with Paul, she felt more despondent than anything else.

When Jim and Betty arrived at the office late that afternoon, Sarah asked them to sit in the waiting room until everyone else had gone home for the day. She then sat next to them and talked a little bit about her apartment. She didn't tell them anything about her new job, just that it was quite far away. They were excited to go and see her apartment. Jim wanted to live someplace that was ten or fewer miles from his job so that the commute would be an easy one, especially in the wintertime. They followed her to her apartment and walked up all of those stairs to the top floor. Jim had to stop once or twice to rest his aching leg. Sarah wondered if the climb would be too much for him until his leg was completely healed.

She bit her lip and asked him, "Jim, I didn't think about your sore leg when I asked if you wanted to see my apartment. Will it be a problem going up and down these stairs twice a day?"

Jim, sweating a little, said with a grimace, "My doctor told me that I needed to get more exercise, especially walking up and down stairs. My leg muscles need to get back into shape. It may be uncomfortable for me at first, but in the long run, climbing these stairs twice a day may cause me to heal faster. Please don't worry about it, Sarah," he said with a little forced grin.

They went inside and looked around the pretty room. Betty exclaimed over how lovely the apartment looked. She looked at Jim with joy and told him that she would love to live there. Jim looked happy and relieved, because he liked the apartment, as well. Sarah had stated that she would leave the furniture and housewares for whoever took over the apartment from her. Jim was amazed to have found a nice home so close to his new job. He offered to pay Sarah for the furniture and other items. They agreed on the reasonable sum of $800. Sarah had loved furnishing the little place over the years, but once she had a more permanent home again, she would enjoy furnishing somewhere new.

Sarah had not had the chance to sort through the two large boxes in her mother's old closet. One box housed all of the Christmas decorations and ornaments that were too dear to give away. Some of the ornaments had been handed down in her mother's family for several generations. In the other large box were several beautiful old quilts that she had inherited from her maternal grandmother. She planned to add her lovely flowered comforter from her bed to that box. She had saved up for months for it, and it was too precious to leave for the new renters. On top of the quilts were other treasures that she had saved from her mother's room.

She hated to ask, but finally did, "May I leave the two boxes that are in the closet here until I come back into the area? It will be a few months before I come back here. When I come back, I will take them with me at that time. Also, the books, CDs, and DVDs on the bookcase are too bulky to take with me. If I let you use them, can they also stay here?"

She hardly dared to believe that Jim and Betty would agree, but was very relieved when Betty said, "Of course, they won't bother us. It will be great to have some music to listen to and movies to watch. I am not much of a reader, but your books will be quite safe staying in the bookcase." Jim nodded in agreement.

"Oh, thank you so much," Sarah sighed with relief.

Sarah told them that she would be taking her two large trunks, suitcase, and backpack with her when she left. She was pretty sure that Susan would keep the trunks safe at her house. Sarah only wanted to take her suitcase, backpack, and purse with her to her new job.

Sarah drove them around the city in her car and said that she would sell it to them for $3000. Jim thought about the nice little nest egg that he had in the bank. He had received a settlement from his car accident, as well as having some savings from his last job. He was saving to get married and for their first house. However, they wanted a small wedding, and he needed a car. He had borrowed his mother's car on Tuesday when he drove to Litton and met Sarah for the first time. Jim and Betty talked it over for a bit and decided to buy it. They questioned Sarah about her move and new job, again, but she basically told them nothing. She just said that she would not need a car for her next job and was happy that someone wanted to buy her little Camry.

Before they left the apartment, Sarah had introduced them to Mrs. Johnson, her landlady. Sarah told her that she would be leaving that weekend, but that Jim would take over the apartment immediately. Sarah had already paid for the October rent, and so Mrs. Johnson did not have much she could say about it. Sarah promised to come back and visit the next time she was in town. She hugged and kissed Mrs. Johnson, who was trying not to cry. Sarah and her mom had lived there for ten years, and Mrs. Johnson was really going to miss her. Sarah told her that she would love having Jim and Betty as tenants.

They had just enough time to get to the Department of Motor Vehicles before it closed for the night. They took care of transferring the title for the car. Sarah took them out for a quick submarine sandwich, and then Jim and Betty went home. Since Sarah still needed the car for Saturday, they agreed to meet at Sarah's apartment on Saturday evening for supper. They would take over the car and apartment at that time.

Sarah had decided to leave most of her furnishings for Jim and Betty. She had the two trunks and a suitcase, and all of her clothes and treasures had to fit into them. She had decided to take only essentials with her to her new job. She lovingly held all of her treasures one last time before carefully putting them in one of the trunks. She put in all of her pictures, the flowered dishes, small china and crystal items, the dried flowers and vase that Paul had given to her on Secretaries Day, her father's blue glass vase, a few wall hangings, her knitting needles and yarn, a lovely decorated tin box, and on the very top, her favorite beautiful flowered mug. In the other trunk, she put in her clothes and a few mementos from her mother. She called Susan and asked if she could come over to see her on Saturday and stay the night. Of course, Susan was happy to have her stay. On Saturday morning, Sarah went to her bank, cashed her last paycheck from her job and Jim's checks for the car and furnishings, took out all of her money, and closed her account. That was it, then. She could leave without a trace.

No, wait, she wanted to go to the cemetery and put flowers on her mom and dad's graves one last time before she left. She did that, sitting on top of her mom's grave and telling them everything, just like she did every Sunday.

"Oh, Mom and Dad, I am so unhappy. You see, I love Paul so much. I know that he is engaged to Belinda, but she is so wrong for him. I would have been a good wife to him. I think that he likes me a little, but he has never hinted that he would ever break up with Belinda. I couldn't bear to see him get married to her. Maybe they will get married while I am away. I guess that I will never know, now. He doesn't want me to work for him anymore. He hired this man named Jim Bacon to take my place. He didn't even talk to me about it. I am so angry with him, even though I will always love him. I need to get away before he comes back from Los Angeles. I don't know if I could keep myself from going to see him if I stayed in town. That's why I have to go far away. I'll be in Brazil. I'm sorry that I won't be able to visit you for a while. They told me that I can come back in three months if I wanted to. I'm going to try and start a new life there. The job seems interesting and the pay is really good. If I worked there for a year or so, I could save up enough money to start over somewhere closer to home. That way I could still come and see you once a month or something. I love you both so much. I know that you want me to be happy. It's just that right now, I don't think that I will ever be happy again. Remember, Mom, how you used to tell me that there would be someone in this big old world who I would find to love? Well, I found him. It's just that he did not find me. I need to go now. I'll think of you every day while I am in Brazil. I'll come and see you in three months. Bye, now," Sarah choked on her tears as she left the cemetery. As she drove away from the cemetery, she told herself that she was doing the right thing by leaving. She longed to see Paul, at least once more, but it would be better for them both if she never saw him again.

After supper with Jim and Betty, Sarah looked around her old home one last time with tears in her eyes. They called a taxi, and when it came, helped her carry her two trunks, backpack, and her suitcase down to the street. Sarah patted her beloved Camry one last time, hugged Jim and Betty, and got into the taxi. The taxi driver put her trunks and suitcase in the trunk and drove away.

It was only a fifteen-minute drive to Susan's home. Sarah got out, paid the driver, included a nice tip, and helped him get her trunks and suitcase onto the sidewalk. Sarah had the backpack and purse over her shoulder. She rang Susan's bell and waited for the door to open. Susan looked at Sarah's pinched and sad face, at her luggage, and just gave her a big hug. She and Sarah lugged all of it indoors. Susan said nothing, but got Sarah a hot beverage and sat down, waiting to hear what she had to say.

Sarah started crying and could not stop for a long time. Susan gave her some tissues and waited some more. At last, Sarah stopped crying and started slowly to tell Susan everything.

"I don't know why Paul wants me to go. He hired Jim to take my place. He couldn't even tell me that he was firing me to my face. What a weasel! Oh, Susan, I love him so much!" Sarah cried. Susan just hugged her and let her talk. When at last Sarah stopped crying and talking, Susan asked a few questions of her own.

"Honey, where are you going? Why can't you just leave your job and get another job around here?" Susan added, "You can move in here, with me. Paul doesn't know me or where I live. Why do you have to leave town?"

Sarah shook her head, "I'm afraid that he would find me or that I would break down and go to see him. No, I must get away from here for a while. I NEED to go away!" Susan just shook her head, unable to believe what was happening.

Sarah asked, "Will you please hang on to my two trunks until I come back? If anything should happen to me, they're yours. Someone would let you know."

Susan's eyes popped right open, staring at Sarah. "What do you mean, Sarah? What could happen to you? Why are you talking this way? Are you sick or something?" Susan asked frantically.

"No, no, nothing like that. I just need to be on my own for a while. I will call you when I can, Susan," soothed Sarah.

After a night of almost no sleep, Sarah got up in the morning, made some hot tea and toast, and then went to shower and change into her travelling clothes. She hugged Susan so hard, cried a little more, and called a taxi. Susan helped her carry her purse, backpack, and suitcase to the taxi, hugged her one more time, and then Sarah got into the taxi and drove away, waving the whole time until the house was out of sight. Sarah got to the airport, boarded her plane, and left the country.

CHAPTER
NINE

Paul couldn't wait to go into the office on Monday morning. He was walking on air. He was back from a successful trip to Los Angeles. But most of all, he wanted to see Sarah and tell her that he had gone to see Belinda and had broken off their engagement on Sunday. It seemed that Belinda was not too upset about it because she had been bored with him. She said that he was never there to take her out when she wanted him to. He worked too many hours at his job and harped too much about having a family. She was not willing to give up the life she enjoyed in order to become 'the little woman'. After complaining to him, for what seemed like forever, about his demand to either get married or break up, she finally said, in a regrettably shrill voice, that she wanted to break up with him.

Paul drove away from her home so relieved that he felt lightheaded. He couldn't believe that he was finally free to talk to Sarah. Sweet little Sarah, how he loved her. He was so scared and nervous because he was not sure if she felt the same way about him as he did about her. Paul wanted to start dating her right away--next week if possible.

The first person he saw when he went into work Monday morning was Jim Bacon, sitting at Sarah's desk. His jaw dropped. He went into his office and saw the envelope that Sarah had left for him on his desk. He looked at it for a long time before slowly reaching out to open it. He read her note slowly and then re-read it, before crushing it in his clenched hand. He felt like someone had plunged a knife into his heart. After seven months of friendship and good working relationship, she had left him with just six lousy little words.

He poked his head out of his office door and asked Jim to come in. Jim came in and sat down in the chair in front of Paul's desk. Paul asked him to explain what he was doing there, and to leave nothing out. Jim told him everything he knew, including that he had bought Sarah's car and had taken over the rent of her home. Paul was shocked and dismayed, but he tried not to let Jim see it. He felt a rage take hold of his heart. He clenched his hands, again, and felt Sarah's note still in his hand. He shakily put it in his pants pocket and willed his breathing to get back to normal.

Paul sent Jim back to his desk and just sat there for the longest time thinking about Sarah and wondering what had gone wrong. He wondered if it had to do with his kiss on their last day together. Or was it because he had hired Jim to take over for her? How he wished that he had warned Jim not to come in or call until the day he was supposed to take over from Sarah. However, it was not Jim's fault; he would have had no reason to suppose that Sarah did not know she was being replaced. Paul took all of the blame on himself, but it did not help assuage his feelings of angst. Paul couldn't concentrate on anything, so he left some instructions for Jim and rushed away from the office. He had to find Sarah.

Paul went to Sarah's old apartment to see if anyone there could tell him anything. No one knew anything about where Sarah had gone. He talked with Mrs. Johnson and asked her for Sarah's new address.

"I don't have one, sir. Sarah said that she got a good new job quite far away. She was sad about leaving here. She and her mom have lived here for more than ten years. They have always been such good tenants. She introduced me to that young Jim Bacon and his girl, Betty. They seem like nice folks. I'm going to miss Sarah. She was such a nice girl. None better," said Mrs. Johnson, sniffing through some tears.

Paul asked her, "Mrs. Johnson, if she stops in to see you, would you let me know? I am worried about her. It just doesn't seem like something that Sarah would do, vanishing like this."

"I will, sir, if she comes to see me," agreed Mrs. Johnson.

Paul wrote down his name and phone number on a little piece of paper and handed it to her. "Thank you, Mrs. Johnson. Bless you," Paul said quietly.

He found out which bank Sarah used and drove himself there, hoping that he could learn something helpful that would tell him where he could find Sarah. He was doomed to be disappointed. Once he arrived there he asked to speak to the manager. Paul knew him slightly. Paul explained that he was Sarah's employer and was concerned about her abrupt departure. He wanted to check up on her and make sure that she was okay. The manager nodded and reviewed his records. He told Paul that she had closed her account and had left no forwarding address.

Paul could not believe that Sarah had vanished without a trace. He talked with all of his employees and anyone he could think of who knew Sarah. He went to the Royal Gardens to see if he could find Clara Burke. After a few hours, he remembered that he had her phone number in his address book. He called Clara. She was shocked to hear that Sarah had left her job and had moved away. Clara was quite disappointed that Sarah had not called her to say goodbye.

"If you hear from her, will you let me know?" Clara asked Paul.

"Yes, I will be glad to do that, Clara. I want to ask you to do the same for me. I care about Sarah, and I need to know that she is safe," Paul told her bleakly. They mutually agreed to call each other if they heard anything from Sarah.

He took the dogs back to the Royal Garden to walk along the paths, desperately hoping that he would see Sarah walking around there. Of course, he had no such luck. He left the Royal Gardens, feeling like he would never go there again. He loved going there on his free Sundays, meeting up with Sarah. He knew that he had fallen in love with her there. This was where he had seen the real Sarah for the first time, all those months ago. He sadly drove home and took his dogs for a very long walk. Then he drove back to Thompson Engineering to pick up the company picture from the shelf in his office. He took it home with him and sat there, looking at her happy pretty face for hours.

Paul's face began to take on a gray and exhausted look, and he started losing weight. He had a hard time sleeping at night and found it difficult to work at his office. His employees started to stay out of his way, for fear that they would get the sharp edge of his tongue. Paul grieved for Sarah, the same as if she had passed away. He did not know if he would ever see her again. He so much wanted the chance to explain, and to see if she could ever forgive him. And maybe, love him just a little.

One day, more than two months after Sarah had gone, Paul was sitting in a restaurant eating supper that he didn't want. He glanced around and saw a smiling young woman sitting with a young man at the table across from him. He stared at her, thinking that he knew her from someplace. It finally dawned on him that he had seen her in Sarah's picture at her home. He had only seen her face a few times, but he had looked at that picture quite thoroughly because Sarah's face was so happy in it. Paul got up and paid his bill. He stopped at Susan's table and excused himself for disturbing them.

He looked at Susan and asked her urgently, "Is your name Susan?" and at her look of enquiry, asked her, "Are you a friend of Sarah Brewster?"

She looked astonished and said, "Yes, my name is Susan. Sarah is my best friend. Who are you, and why do you want to know about Sarah?"

Paul said, "My name is Paul Thompson. Could I talk with you for a few minutes?"

Susan, who knew that this was Sarah's Paul, talked quietly and briefly with her date. He left quickly, so she asked Paul to sit down. Paul did not want to talk about Sarah in a public restaurant, so he asked her if they could talk somewhere private. Not wanting to scare her, he asked if she would talk with him in his car. He stressed that it was on a well-lit street. Susan smiled at that and agreed to talk with him. Paul asked if he could pay her bill, and then they went out to his car.

He settled her into his car and sat for a minute, trying to find the words.

Finally, Susan said, "I know who you are. Sarah told me all about you. Why are you asking about her? I was told that you were engaged to a woman named Belinda." She looked at him with a frown.

He stared at her and then told her that he had broken his engagement with Belinda on the Sunday that he came back to work from his trip to Los Angeles. Susan looked surprised and quite unhappy.

She said with difficulty, "Sarah left for her new job that Sunday, and I have not heard from her since."

Paul felt all of his hopes die at that moment. "So, you don't know where she is?" he whispered tragically. "I just can't believe that she is gone! I planned to tell her that I loved her on that Monday. I came back from Los Angeles so happy and full of plans for us, to find that she had gone before I could get there. She left me a note," he spoke bleakly. "She only said goodbye and to have a happy life," he said brokenly. "As if I could have a happy life without her in it," Paul said bitterly. "I never got the chance to tell her that I love her. Oh, Susan, what am I going to do?" Paul asked her as tears came into his eyes. Susan put her hand on his sleeve in sympathy. She decided to ask Paul to come to the house so they could talk some more.

The first thing he saw was the identical picture to Sarah's, in which she and Susan were smiling with their arms around each other. He looked at it for a long time, his face becoming sad and white. Susan asked him to sit down and got him a cup of coffee. They talked about Sarah for half an hour. Susan could see Paul's extreme sadness and decided to tell him about Sarah's last evening with her. Paul felt his heart lurch when Susan told him that Sarah left because she loved him and could not face seeing him married to Belinda. He smiled for the first time in two months.

"Oh, Sarah, where are you?" he silently wondered. Now he really wanted the chance to explain his actions to her. If they could just find her, maybe she would forgive him and come back. He started questioning Susan even more thoroughly. Susan mentioned that she had Sarah's two trunks in her closet.

"Do you think that I could look in them and see if there is any clue to her whereabouts?" Paul asked her hesitantly.

Susan looked thoughtful and said, "I didn't think about doing that. Sarah told me that if anything were to happen to her, they would belong to me. I have been so afraid that she might be sick or dying somewhere without anyone she loves around her." Paul just stared at her, horrified, and his face got even whiter.

They hauled out the trunks and pulled them up to the couch and looked into the first one. They could see that it was mostly clothing, so they closed it and opened the other one. The first thing that Paul saw, sitting on the top, was Sarah's beautiful flowered mug. His face went ash white.

"Oh, no! That is Sarah's favorite mug. She told me several times that it goes wherever she goes." He could not stop his voice from shaking. Here was proof that something was very wrong. Sarah would have taken her favorite mug with her to a new job. Why had she left it behind, and why had she said that bit to Susan about her trunks going to her if anything happened to Sarah?

They carefully unpacked all of Sarah's treasures and looked over each item. When Paul pulled out the dried flowers in the vase that he had given Sarah, he held them for a few seconds, just remembering that day. He had been happy to give his delightfully sunny Sarah flowers on Secretaries Day. He knew how much she loved them. She had kept them on her desk for a week until they started to really wilt and dry up. He had thought that she had thrown them away, but it seems that she had kept them and put them with her other treasures. That soothed his ravaged heart for just a moment.

Susan pulled out the old-fashioned black velvet ring box and opened it. She looked at the empty box and said slowly, "Sarah's mother's ring is missing. I wonder where it is. I wonder if she sold it. No, that can't be it, she would only sell it if she was desperate. That means she must have it with her." Susan sat, remembering, "It was so silly, we pretended that we were married ladies. Sarah put on her mom's wedding dress and her ring. The ring was a bit too small because her mom had such small hands. Sarah had to use soap and really pull at it to get it off her finger. I don't think she ever tried it on again. Now, why is it not in its box?"

Susan stopped talking and said, "I'm sorry, I should stop talking. You probably don't want to hear all of this. This was just silliness between two very good friends. I was helping her go through all of her mom's belongings about a month after she died. We were laughing and crying, just remembering Mrs. Brewster."

Paul smiled sadly at her and said, "No, please go on. I want to know about Sarah. You are her best friend. You know her better than anyone else in the world. Talking about her brings her closer to me."

So, Susan talked about how they had met when they were nine years old. Sarah's father had recently been killed in a car accident as he and their dog, Wolfie, were on the way to the vet's office. They had been hit head-on, and both Mr. Brewster and Wolfie had died immediately. There was not a lot of money, so after the funeral and outstanding bills had been paid, Sarah and her mom had been forced to sell their house and move into a dinky little apartment about two blocks from Susan's house. On the first day at her new school, Sarah had come into the classroom with her pigtails and pink dress, looking very sad. Paul felt a pang for that little girl who was so sad and lost.

Susan had liked Sarah right away. "We were both girlie girls," she told him. That meant that they both liked everything pretty, pink, and glitzy. Sarah, it seemed, always wore pink or green, her two favorite colors. She liked long swirly, flowery skirts and pretty tops. Paul thought, with a tender smile, that she still liked them the best.

Susan told him how Sarah and her mother always invited her over to their apartment when things were heating up at her home. When she was fourteen, Susan's parents went through a difficult and nasty divorce. Susan said that she spent more time at Sarah's apartment than at her own home. She said loyally that Sarah and her mom were the sweetest and best friends that any person could ever have. That is why she would do anything for Sarah. Paul felt like he had been given a gift, to have glimpsed just a slice of Sarah's life as a young girl.

They continued to take Sarah's treasures out of the trunk. Susan found Sarah's tiny perfect crystal unicorn. "Oh, she still has this, after all these years. I gave this to Sarah for her birthday the year that my parents got divorced. It was quite expensive, but my mom and I wanted to show Sarah and Mrs. Brewster how thankful we were for always letting me hang out with them when it was so hard to be at home. I haven't seen it in years. I thought that it had gotten lost or broken."

Susan touched the unicorn gently and put it back in its tiny box. At the bottom of the trunk was a beautifully decorated tin box. When they opened it, they immediately saw a bunch of money, mostly one-hundred-dollar bills. At the bottom of the box were Sarah's personal papers, bank statements, credit card bills, and such. Susan counted the money and was shocked to discover that there was in excess of $8,000 in there.

"Wow, I never knew that Sarah had this kind of money," she breathed. "When did she make all of this money? She must have taken only a small amount with her, wherever she went."

Paul said thoughtfully, "Well, she emptied her bank account, and sold her car and furniture to my new secretary. She could have been saving her money for a while. I wonder how much money she took with her." He frowned, "How can she have moved somewhere else with no car, no furniture, none of her treasures, and hardly any money?"

"Susan, are you sure that she didn't tell you anything that we can use to find her?" Susan shook her head no. Everything was out of the trunk, but they could find no clue as to where she had gone. They carefully packed everything back up and put the trunks back into Susan's closet.

Susan felt better after talking with Paul, and she knew that he loved Sarah with all his heart. When he asked her if he could call her again to talk about Sarah, she agreed. He gave her his private phone number and told her that she could call him anytime day or night if she had news of Sarah.

He hesitantly asked, "If she calls you, will you tell her that I found you and that we talked? I would like to see her sweet face when I tell her that I love her, but if you do talk with her, will you tell her, please? I don't know if she ever wants to see me again, but if she knows that I am free of Belinda and that I love her, she might decide to come home."

Susan took one look at his haggard face and agreed to call him and let him know if Sarah called her. She also agreed to tell Sarah about Paul's freedom and his love. With tears in his eyes, he touched her shoulder and said goodnight. He walked away and closed the door softly on his way out.

Paul went home and took his dogs for a long walk. He had a lot to think about. He was so worried about Sarah. He wondered if she had found out that she had a terminal illness or something. He would do anything, even give up his company, if it meant that he could see her and talk with her again. He loved her with every fiber of his being and longed to hold her in his arms and talk with her. If she was very sick, he would do anything in the world for her, to either cure her or just spend whatever time she had left with her. He needed to be with her, to talk to, to hold, to love.

Paul let himself back into his home, after a long exhausting walk. Even Mutt and Jeff were dragging their doggy feet. He wiped their paws and bedded them down for the night. He got himself a hot beverage and went into his living room to relax. The weather was right for a nice fire in the fireplace. Paul put on some beautiful, but sad, music and sat down in his comfortable leather chair in front of the fireplace. He let the music wash over him. He thought about Sarah and the pleasant life they would have had if she were still here. He had to come to grips with the fact that he might never see Sarah again. Because of his exhaustion, the sad music, and his even sadder thoughts, tears came into his eyes and slowly rolled down his cheeks. He let them fall; no one would see them. The catharsis was painful, yet oddly left him with a feeling of peace. The only other time in his life that he had felt his emotions as deeply was when his father had passed away. He knew now that, given the opportunity, Sarah would know that she was more important than any other person--or thing--in his life. He took himself up to bed and slept deeply for the first time in several months. He woke up the next morning, remembering his dream about Sarah.

In his crystal-clear dream, he was experiencing his tenth anniversary married to Sarah. Their two sons and small daughter were helping him fill the room with flowers for Sarah. They were to renew their wedding vows that afternoon in their home. It felt so real that he woke up smiling. He felt that God was reassuring him that he would have Sarah back in his life. And what a life! He hoped that he would continue this dream tonight. He wished that he could tell Sarah about this wonderful dream.

CHAPTER

TEN

There was something niggling at the back of Susan's mind. She knew that it was regarding Sarah. Finally, a week later, when she was watching a travel show on her television, she remembered. "Her passport! Her passport was not in the tin box with the rest of her important papers." Since Paul and she had not seen it, that must mean that Sarah had taken it with her. But why? Did Sarah leave the country? She thought that Paul might want to know this information.

The phone rang. Paul looked at the caller ID and saw that it was Susan's number. He snatched up the phone after only one ring. "Hello, Susan," he spoke urgently into the phone.

"Paul, I just thought of something. Sarah's passport was not in the trunk with her other important documents. I know she has one because she and I went to England three years ago. Why would she take her passport with her unless she was planning to leave the country?" Susan enquired.

Paul thought for a few seconds before replying, "Maybe she just wanted to have another form of ID on her."

Susan asked him if he knew anything about Sarah knowing someone living in another country. Paul said that he didn't know anything about that. Their conversations had never included talking about anyone who lived outside of the United States.

"Susan, do you think that she left here to go somewhere overseas?" Paul asked, anxiously.

Susan did not really think that Sarah would go so far as to leave the country, but it was something that they should keep in mind. They chatted comfortably for a few more minutes before Paul asked if he could meet her for coffee the next day. Susan told him to come over to her place for coffee after supper. He agreed to come over around 7:00 pm.

After Paul hung up, he decided to go tomorrow to Petal's Bakery on Rosemont Street. He had stopped there many times to pick up treats for family gatherings since he was not a baker nor a good cook. He always enjoyed talking with Petal, the bakery's namesake, and her father. It was her father's idea to name the bakery after his little 'flower', an obvious pun that he could not resist. They made the most scrumptious snickerdoodle cookies in the world. It was their specialty cookie. Susan laughingly told him that she and Sarah both had a passion for homemade snickerdoodles. Susan had been so nice and helpful when they met. He was grateful to her for talking with him about Sarah. He knew that Susan would help him in any way that she could. They both loved Sarah and would do anything for her.

After a long day at work, Paul was looking forward to dropping by Susan's home. He had completed quite a lot of work that day. This past week, ever since his wonderful dream about Sarah, he had gone to work in a better frame of mind. His employees were so happy to see him looking better and more energetic than he had looked for several months. They still did not know his story, or Sarah's, and had wondered what had happened to make him so lost and despondent over the past several months. They figured that it had something to do with Sarah. He still treated them all with his usual courtesy and thoughtfulness, but the joy had gone from his soul. He had gotten much closer to all of them during those two months after the picnic and before Sarah had left suddenly. Now they were hopeful that he would resume his good working relationship with them. That morning, Paul brought in several dozen assorted homemade cookies from Petal's Bakery and put them in the break room for everyone to enjoy. He kept a dozen snickerdoodles in his car to take over to Susan's house that evening.

Munching on a chocolate chip cookie in his office, Paul dictated a letter to Jim Bacon, accepting an offer to speak at a workshop in a month's time. Jim couldn't stop his grin when Paul accidentally sprayed cookie crumbs all over his desk while he was talking. Instead of frowning or going ballistic, Paul just started laughing.

"Oh, it was so good to hear him laugh," thought Jim. Jim had not had an easy start to his job. Paul had been upset since Jim's very first day at work. Somehow, Jim had decided that he was to blame for Paul's change in behavior. After talking with the other bewildered employees, Jim had gotten the idea that Paul had only been unhappy and brooding since he started working. Hearing Paul laugh made Jim feel that things would start getting better at the job. Jim had felt so bad about his job that he had considered quitting. The only thing that caused him to stay was that Betty loved their new apartment, and the money was better than any job he had ever had. He thought about their small wedding two weeks ago. He had not even felt that he could ask Paul for time off for a honeymoon. Now, with Paul feeling better, Jim decided to ask him for a week off so that he could take Betty on the honeymoon that she deserved.

Paul left his office in a decent mood. He had started to take up the reins of his working life, again. Everything had been on hold for more than two months while he was dealing with his depression over Sarah's departure. He grinned at the memory of his laughter when he accidentally spit his cookie crumbs all over his desk. Jim had looked apprehensively at Paul for a quick moment until Paul laughed. Jim's grin had made Paul feel even better. Paul realized that Jim had had a difficult time with his job. No one had told Jim why Paul was so unhappy. Paul thought that he would have to have a little talk with Jim tomorrow and try to make up for the past several months. Feeling better than he felt in months, he drove to Susan's house. He rang the doorbell, cookies in hand. She opened it and saw the cookies.

"Oh, what kind are they?" was the first thing she asked.

"Snickerdoodles, of course," he replied. "They are the best snickerdoodles that I personally have ever tasted," he proclaimed.

"Oh, you dear man!" Susan exclaimed, throwing her arms around his neck. They both laughed as they advanced into her kitchen. It felt good to feel halfway normal, again, Paul thought. Susan grinned and helped herself to a cookie.

"I've already had supper, so it's okay if I have dessert," she said, with her mouth full.

Paul laughed and told her how he had sprayed cookie crumbs all over his desk that afternoon while he was dictating a letter to Jim. Susan laughed and helped herself to a second cookie. Paul reached for one, too. They went into the living room and Paul told her all about his dream, and what a difference that had made in his life. He told her that he felt that God had let him know that he would see Sarah, again, and that she would be in his life. He told her about the two little boys and a sweet little girl that they had in his dream.

Susan smiled hugely and said, "I hope that you named your daughter after me. After all, I am Sarah's best friend." Paul smiled and said that he would keep that in mind to talk about with Sarah, the minute that they found out that she was pregnant. He could not stop grinning at that thought. It would be the most incredible thing in his life, after his wedding to Sarah. He hoped with his whole being that it would not be just a dream but a reality in his future.

ELEVEN

Sarah got off the plane in Brazil. The air outside the airport was warm and humid, even in early October. She looked around and could see the mountains in the distance. Coming towards her at a fast pace, was an older jeep. Inside the jeep, she saw a middle-aged man and woman. The jeep pulled up next to her.

"Are you Sarah Brewster?" asked the woman.

"Yes, I'm Sarah." They looked at her and her suitcase. "Is that everything you have?" the woman asked.

Sarah pointed to her backpack and purse, which were slung over her shoulder, and stated, "Yes, the suitcase and these two are the only things I brought with me. Don't you think it will be enough?"

The man laughed and said, "Well, if you were Mary, here, you would have at least twice that amount. I wish that Mary could pack as frugally as you seem to have done."

Mary laughingly hit him on the shoulder and said, "Never mind my husband, you obviously know how to pack lightly." Mary introduced herself, "My name is Mary Edwards. This lunkhead is my husband, Ted. He's the manager at the mine. I'm the main cook. We're here to pick you up and bring you back with us. Do you have everything? If so, we should get going." Ted got out of the jeep and put Sarah's suitcase on the back seat.

"Jump in," he invited Sarah. She did, and the jeep took off at a great rate. Sarah felt like she was on some kind of an amusement ride.

The compound that they drove into was very clean and neat. There was a large building, surrounded on one side by eight barracks. On the other side were three cottages. The largest was the home where the Edwards lived. In the cottage next to them lived the doctor. A small surgery/clinic was attached to his cottage. The last in the row, the smallest cottage, was to be the home that Sarah would share with the general helper. Mary told Sarah about her new roommate. She was a thirty-year-old woman named Trish, who helped out with anything that needed to be done. She helped Mary cook the meals and clean up and went wherever she was needed most.

They went first into the main building. Sarah's job was to do all of the secretarial work. That included payroll, making out any spreadsheets or checklists that were needed, and just about anything that needed to be done in an office. The building included an up-to-date office, with all of the newest electronic and computer equipment. Ted's office was there, as well as Sarah's desk, and a good-sized waiting room.

Through a door was the cafeteria. It was large enough to seat forty people at one time. There were five large rectangular tables set up with eight chairs at each table. Next to the cafeteria was the large kitchen, where Mary and Trish made all of the meals. Through another door was a large recreation room. In it were couches, small tables with chairs, a pool table, and several dartboards on the walls. In one corner were a few vending machines, a soft drink dispenser, and a large bookcase which held a variety of board games, CDs, DVDs, and books. There was a large screen TV with a stereo set up on a wooden entertainment center in front of the largest couch. In another corner, Sarah could see a few washing machines and dryers next to a long narrow table. She supposed that was where they would all do their laundry. She did not look forward to washing her clothes in the same machines in which the miners would be washing their grimy clothes.

Once you went out the back door, you could see the eight barracks that housed the miners. Each barrack housed up to four miners. Currently, there were only twenty-five men living and working there.

Sarah looked at the entrance to the mine, which was about a quarter of a mile to the rear of the barracks. The miners worked from 9:00 am until 5:00 pm five days a week. They had every weekend off and could leave the compound if they wanted. Those who stayed at the compound relaxed in their barracks or in the recreation room. The mining company tried to make them as comfortable as possible so that they would stay on.

Everyone who worked for the mine signed a three-month contract. At the end of three months, they were either free to leave or sign another contract for a further three months. Many of the miners had lived and worked there for a good many years. Mary and Ted had lived there for five years, and the doctor had just been there for a year. Trish had lived and worked there for eighteen months. Sarah was the newbie. The secretary that she was replacing had left after six months because she couldn't stand the quietness of her life there. Everyone hoped that Sarah would like it and stay for a while. It was difficult to have to keep training in someone new all of the time.

Mary and Ted took Sarah into her new home. The cottage was small, but it was bigger than Sarah's last apartment. There were two small bedrooms and a bathroom with a shower and a bathtub. Sarah was happy to see that. When she had free time, she liked to take a bubble bath. In between the two bedrooms was a living/dining room, complete with everything that they would need to live comfortably. A vertical compact washer and dryer, one on top of the other, were squished into the last remaining space in an alcove. Sarah felt relief when she saw them. She would not have to wash her clothes in the recreation hall with the miners.

Out of one of the bedrooms came Trish. She was a small and wiry woman with thick curly brown hair that she had tied back in a short ponytail. She was dressed in a type of uniform--a dark green overall, with a tan shirt under it. Trish had a nice freckled face and was smiling at them.

"Hello, and welcome to your new home. You must be Sarah. I'm Trish Newburg. I will be your new roommate, at least for three months. Hopefully, you will like it here and decide to stay longer. I'm saving as much money as I can. If I stay for a few more years, I will have enough to move back to Iowa and open my own business."

Sarah shook hands with her and smiled. "Let me put my things away, and then you can show me the ropes." Sarah went into her bedroom and looked around. "Home, sweet home, for the next three months," she told herself softly.

Mary, Ted, Trish, and Sarah walked back to the office. There they met Dave, the doctor. He was a tall thin young man, about thirty years old. He wore thick black glasses and had fly-away curly blond hair. He smiled at them all, especially at Sarah, because she looked a bit nervous. They introduced themselves and everyone sat down in the comfortable chairs. They invited Sarah to tell them about herself. She looked down at her mother's ring on her hand and started to weave an interesting story about her life, including the newly made-up fiance, Paul, who was a doctor and currently living in Africa working with Doctors Without Borders.

Before she left the United States, Sarah had decided that she would present herself as a newly engaged woman, who was sad because she was missing her fiance. He was a dedicated young doctor who wanted to get as much experience as possible, so he joined Doctors Without Borders. He was going to be in Africa for six months or so. Sarah had come up with this story to protect her from unwanted attention from the miners and co-workers. She was in love with Paul and had no desire to meet and date anyone else. Later, if she felt differently, she could always say that she and Paul decided to go their separate ways. At this point in time, she did not think that she would ever get over Paul and want to have a relationship with any other man, so being engaged to a man who could not be there, suited her very well.

Sarah talked about her relationship with Paul and how much they loved each other. Paul wanted to experience working with the Doctors Without Borders group before he settled into a job at a hospital. They had agreed that they could handle being apart for a few months so that Paul could have that experience. Sarah finally stopped to take a breath. She looked at the smiling faces of the others and felt ready to go on with her life. They spent time telling Sarah their own stories. After two hours, they all felt that they knew each other much better.

Mary and Trish left to make supper; Dave left to do something at his clinic. That left Ted to show Sarah around the office and explain all of her duties to her. They worked until the supper bell sounded, then went next door to the cafeteria to meet the miners and sit down for the evening meal. Sarah sat at a table with Ted and Dave. She stood up and introduced herself to all of the miners who were sitting in groups of seven or eight at the other tables. She looked at their smiles and nods and felt that at least she would be around other people, so she would not have a chance to be lonely. She forgot that you can be surrounded by other people and still feel lonely.

Sarah learned her job well. She was creative and intelligent. She helped Ted set up new and inventive spreadsheets and made some brochures for the company. It was only at night when she lay snug in her little bedroom at the cottage that she could not stop thinking about Paul. She wondered if he was married by now. She thought about Jim Bacon and his Betty. Were they married? Did they like living in her old apartment? Then she thought about Clara and Rip. Did they still go to the Royal Garden and meet up with Paul and his dogs? Was anyone putting flowers on her parents' graves? It all rolled around and around in her head. Sometimes she found it impossible to sleep at night. After a night of restless tossing, she would get up and know that she did not look her best. She would drop a hint about missing Paul, and then everyone would be kind and leave her to get on with her work.

Despite her unhappiness, Sarah found the work interesting. She had a natural flair for computers, and she enjoyed learning new programs and applications from Dave and Ted. She got along with everyone, just as she had always done at every job she had ever had. Sarah was surprised and pleased at how much she and Trish had in common. They both liked to knit and bake. They liked the same type of movies and books. Trish liked Country music, whereas Sarah liked classical music and soft rock. Even so, they listened to each other's music at times, and it helped them to grow in appreciation for the other.

The owner of the mine and the compound was an attractive millionaire named Senor Carlos Santos. Five years ago, he had deputized Ted to do all of the hiring for the company. Senor Santos liked to visit the compound five or six times a year. He had his own small plane and would fly himself to the mine. The small airfield was on the far side of the mine. A jeep was always waiting in the hangar for his use while he was at the mine. He had regular meetings with Ted, sometimes on-site, and other times they were conference or video calls. He had known Mary and Ted Edwards for five years and had met Dave and Trish when they arrived, as well. Some of the miners had been there for many years and were on very good terms with him. Senor Santos liked to keep his employees happy, so he made the compound as comfortable as possible. Sarah was at her desk working on her daily work when he came in one day. She had been working for the company for exactly one month. Sarah recognized him from the picture that hung on the wall in the waiting room.

"Good morning, Senor Santos," Sarah said in her soft and pleasant voice. Senor Santos looked quickly at her and just stared at her. He liked what he saw. He was immediately attracted to Sarah.

"Ola," he said, still looking at her. He knew who she was because Ted had sent him her resume and a quick update on Sarah when she started at the company. "Você é muito charmosa," he said softly to her. Sarah blushed prettily and looked down at her desk. She had privately been learning some Portuguese in her own time, and she knew that he had told her that she was very charming. She put out her hand to shake his hand. She thought that Senor Santos was quite attractive for an older gentleman. She knew that he was forty-five years old and unmarried. Sarah did not want any entanglements with any men while she was in Brazil. She was very much in love with Paul.

Senor Santos had been told by Ted that Sarah was engaged to be married. Now that he had met her, he was disappointed, but at least she was not yet married. He wanted to get to know her better. He sat down in front of her and proceeded to ask her questions about her work and her private life. Sarah felt quite uncomfortable because she could feel his interest in her. There was no way that she wanted to get involved with Senor Santos in a romantic way. On the other hand, she did not want to jeopardize her job. Sarah told him general tidbits of information regarding her past jobs. She shyly talked about Paul. Senor Santos was intrigued by her shyness and her natural appearance. He liked demure and gentle women. He left her to talk with Ted for an hour.

At lunchtime, he went with them into the dining room. He immediately sat down with a few of the miners that he knew quite well. There was quite a bit of laughter at his table all through the lunch hour. Sarah watched him in surprise. He was much nicer than she had thought he would be. Senor Santos finished eating with the miners and then came over to where Sarah, Dave, and Ted were sitting.

He asked Sarah, "Miss Sarah, I would like to take you out to eat on my next visit, if you will allow that. It is always good to spend a little time away from the mine and your responsibilities. Now, don't get upset. I know that you are engaged to be married. I just want the chance to talk with you and show my appreciation to you for the good work that you are doing. What do you say? I will be back for a quick visit in a month. Think about it, okay?" Sarah looked at him and was not sure what she should say to him.

She did not want to anger him, so she quietly said, "I will think about it, Senor Santos. It was very nice to meet you today."

He smiled at her with great charm, turned to Ted, and said, "Ted, I will need to talk with you for a little while longer. Will you meet me in your office in half an hour?" Ted smiled and agreed. Sarah did not see Senor Santos again on that particular trip.

They were given company uniforms to wear in the office. The pants and skirts were dark green, while the pullovers and shirts were tan with a dark green logo of the company on the front.

Because she wore her uniform during the week, Sarah only needed to wear her own clothes in the evenings and on weekends. Even so, she began to get very tired of the clothes that she had brought with her.

"I am so tired of my clothes," Sarah complained lightly to Trish one evening.

Trish looked up from the sweater that she was knitting and said, "You know, we could get permission to use the jeep and go into town this coming weekend to go shopping. I am just about ready to give away everything I have here and get some new clothes, too. I've been here a lot longer than you have, my friend. What do you think? Do you want to ask Ted and Mary if they want to go with us?"

"Yes," she said with enthusiasm. "Let's go over right now to Mary's cottage and ask her if they want to go with us," Sarah said with a big smile.

Mary was just as excited to go shopping as they were. She said that she would have to talk with Ted, who was meeting with Dave at the moment. She said that she would let them know in the morning.

The next morning in the office, Mary and Ted told Sarah that they would love to go into Ouro Preto, a university town about fifty miles away. They decided to stay the night in a small hotel, so they would have all day to shop on Saturday and a leisurely day of sightseeing on Sunday. Sarah was excited to see a little of Brazil. So far, she had not budged off of the compound.

Trish, Sarah, Mary, and Ted set out early on Saturday morning. Dave stayed behind, just in case any of the miners needed anything. He had given Trish a list of goodies to get for him, though. The friends set off, in a lighthearted mood, for their little mini holiday.

Mary wanted to go out to eat as soon as they got into town. She was tired of eating her own food. Brazil had such a rich variety of gastronomic delights.

Mary told the others, "I'm going to have feijoada, which is one of Brazil's most famous dishes. It's a hearty black bean and mixed meat stew." Mary's mouth watered just talking about it.

Sarah could not wait to try it and said, "I'll try that, too. I was reading up about Brazilian food and found that it is often served with a tomato and lettuce salad. That's what I am going to have. What about you, Trish?" Trish thought that she would have the same.

Ted said, "It's unanimous, then. Feijoada for everyone. Allow me to pick out the wine. Mary and I found a great little wine that goes well with this meal the last time we were here." They all thought that it was an excellent idea. They all ate their meal in the best of spirits.

They headed out to the shopping areas. Sarah loved all of the colorful women's clothing that she saw. She hadn't spent any money as yet in Brazil, so she felt justified in parting with her hard- earned cash. Sarah bought two new skirts and three very pretty tops and some knitting needles and colorful yarn, along with a pattern for a warm chunky sweater. She doubted if she would have it finished before her three months were completed. Trish and Mary bought some new clothes as well. Mary tried to talk Ted into getting some new clothes, but he just laughed.

"It figures that you women want new clothes. Don't you know by now that we men like our old clothes? Who wants to have to break in new ones? Not me. I'm just fine as I am, woman," he said in a teasing voice to Mary.

She just shook her head at him but didn't press him to buy anything. They walked past a hair salon and Sarah decided on the spot to have her hair cut. She found that the hairstylist could see her immediately. She sent the others on to finish their shopping while she sat in the salon. She decided to have fourteen inches cut off the length of her hair. She left the salon with a completely new look. Her waist-long hair was now a shiny and elegant shoulder-length bob. She had never had hair that short. Even as a young girl, her hair had always been long. Mary and Ted exclaimed over Sarah's new look.

Ted grinned and said, "Your Paul might not even recognize you, Sarah. You better send him a quick photo of you, showing off your new look."

Sarah's lips quivered as she heard that. Trish, seeing her sudden sadness, gave her a hug and told her that she looked fabulous and that Paul was going to love her new hairdo. Sarah felt herself being pulled along the street, arm in arm with Trish. They spent the rest of the day looking in shops and buying everything they had on their lists. Sarah, well satisfied with the day's shopping, fell into her comfortable hotel bed and dreamed about Paul. She dreamt that they were sitting on their deck, playing with their two little boys and tiny little daughter. They would stop playing with the babies every so often and just look into each other's eyes, totally in love with each other, even after years of marriage. She woke up crying, wishing with all of her heart that that dream would come true. As it was, she didn't think that she would ever see Paul again. He would never see her new haircut, she thought sadly.

On Sunday the four friends looked at the university and as many museums as they could fit in before they had to start driving back to the camp. It had been a wonderful weekend, and it rejuvenated them. They all felt relaxed and ready to take up their somewhat monotonous lives again.

Over time, Sarah lost about fifteen pounds. She was now quite slender. She went for long walks and didn't always eat as much as she should. Her mom's ring wasn't tight on her finger anymore. She liked her new haircut. It was very easy to take care of. She usually still wore a ponytail for work, but sometimes she just let it hang, silky and shining on her shoulders.

She and Trish were now firm friends. Trish told Sarah all about the yarn and knitting shop that she hoped to open in her hometown in Iowa when she went back there to live. She had left Iowa to escape a love affair that had gone wrong. Her fiance had cheated on her, she told Sarah. Trish had fled from her hometown without ever confronting her fiance. She had been so hurt that she just had to get away. Sarah thought about Trish's situation a lot. Hadn't she done almost the same thing? As much as she was tempted to tell Trish about Paul and the real reason that she had come to Brazil, she didn't think she could bear to talk about it, yet. Trish never told Sarah that she heard her crying at night. By the same token, Sarah never told Trish that she heard her crying in the night, as well. In the evenings, after supper, they often sat in their tiny living room, knitting and listening to music, talking when it suited them. How funny to think that months ago Paul had envisioned Sarah doing that very thing on an evening at home.

A month after Senor Santos had made his last visit, he came again. Sarah was the first to see him again.

"Ola, Sarah. Have you decided to let me take you out for a meal? Ouro Preto is only an hour's drive from here. Or we could go farther afield if you don't mind flying in my small plane. I hope that you will agree to come with me. Eu gosto muito de você," he said softly to her.

She knew that he liked her. She said pleasantly to him, "Senor Santos, as long as you understand that I am engaged to be married,

I will have a meal with you. I don't really care for flying, but I would agree to drive to Ouro Preto with you. A few of us drove there a month ago, and I really liked the town."

He looked at her with his dark passionate eyes and smiled nicely. "I will be a perfect gentleman. It will be good for my image to be seen with such a lovely young woman," he spoke gently to her.

They left as soon as she finished her work for the day. On the way to Ouro Preto, he kept up an amusing dialogue with Sarah. He had many humorous stories about places that he had visited and people he knew. He looked at Sarah quite often while he drove. She really was a sweet and pretty young woman, he decided.

"When did you cut your hair, Amorzinho?" he asked her. Sarah told him more about her weekend getaway with Trish, Mary, and Ted.

He smiled nicely and told her, "I preferred your long beautiful hair, but no matter, it will grow long again."

Sarah did not say anything to that. She thought that he was being too familiar with her. After all, she was one of his employees, and this was only the second time that they had met. Senor Santos took Sarah to an expensive restaurant where he was well-known. Their table and the service were beyond reproach. Sarah found herself relaxing and ended up having a nice time. Senor Santos was a perfect gentleman. His manners were lovely, and he knew so many people. She saw the raised eyebrows on a few of the couples who greeted them. Senor Santos politely introduced her to them just as Sarah Brewster, without any other explanation. After their meal, he drove around the town for an hour before starting on his way back to the mine. Once back at the mine, he held her hands in his, and just looked at her for several minutes.

"Thank you for a wonderful evening, Miss Sarah. I hope that you will allow me to take you out again, the next time I visit," he spoke softly to her. Sarah smiled shyly and nodded her head, not knowing what to say. "Good night, Amorzinho," he told her as he leaned over and gently kissed her cheek.

She told him good night in her soft voice and turned away to go to her cabin. Once inside, she told Trish, who had waited up to ask about her evening, that Senor Santos had been a very nice date and that she had enjoyed the little outing. Trish thought that it was about time that Sarah had a night out, instead of sitting in her bedroom staring at Paul's picture until she finally slept. Ted and Mary were also happy that Sarah had a nice time with Senor Santos. They all wanted Sarah to feel better about being there. They wanted her to re-sign her contract and spend the next three months with them.

As the end of her three-month contract loomed near, Sarah really had to think about what she wanted to do. She had built a new life here, but she missed her old home and friends so much. She still thought about Paul every day and hoped that, somehow, he had figured out how to be happy again. She kept thinking about the last time they had met and how sad and dejected he had seemed. She replayed his kiss in her mind a thousand times. She knew that he had not meant to kiss her; it just happened before he could prevent it. She had put the picture of Paul in a silver frame, and it sat on the end table in her bedroom. She knew every single pore and eyelash on his dear face, after looking at it night after night, sometimes for hours.

Sarah felt that it would be safe to go back home and visit Susan. It was a big town. There was no reason to believe that she would run into Paul or one of her other friends while she was visiting Susan. She wished she could find out about Jim Bacon and Betty. But how could she do that without alerting Paul to the fact that she was back? Jim worked for Paul now, and might accidentally let slip the news that she was back in town to him. Sarah wanted to go to the cemetery to visit her parents. She missed that old ritual every Sunday.

With two weeks left in her contract, Sarah finally told them that she wanted to fly back to her home for a visit. She wanted a week off. After a week, she would either decide to resign and stay there, or she would come back and sign a contract for another three months. Ted, Mary, Dave, and Trish had all become her good friends by now. They understood that she needed to go back and spend a week at home. They thought that Paul would be there, visiting from Africa, as well. They all wished that she would decide to come back for another three months, though.

Sarah packed up her suitcase, backpack, and purse. She said goodbye to her friends at the airport. They all had packed into the jeep to see her off. After several rounds of hugs and kisses, Sarah walked away and got onto the plane. During the flight, she spared a quick thought for Senor Santos. She wondered if he would be upset if she decided not to go back to the mine. She had promised Mary that she would call them at the end of the week and let them know if she would be coming back or not.

Sarah had arranged to stay overnight at the hotel next to the airport. After a good night's sleep, she would call Susan to tell her that she was back in Litton. Susan would be at work until 4:00 pm.

Sarah planned the next day carefully--lunch at the nearby mall, shopping to buy some warmer clothes, and then a visit to her parents' graves. That should fill the day until she could call Susan.

CHAPTER
TWELVE

The plane landed amid a snowy evening. Sarah shivered as she waited for the hotel shuttle. Tomorrow, she would have to buy a warmer coat and some boots. She got into her room and took a hot shower. The bed looked very inviting. She curled up and fell asleep almost at once.

She woke up at 9:30 am. After showering again, she went down to the coffee shop in the hotel lobby and had a cup of coffee and a bagel with cream cheese and raspberry jam. Once again in her room, she watched TV until it was time to check out at 11:00 am.

At the mall, Sarah took a good look around. Because it was after Christmas, there were many sales going on. For a weekday at lunchtime, it was very busy. Several hours later, with more packages than she planned to have, she took a taxi to the nursery where she used to buy her Sunday flowers each week. From there, she went to her old church. She talked the priests' secretary into letting her pile her things in the closet behind the desk.

Sarah took her flowers and went into the cemetery. After putting the flowers on her parent's graves and chatting for as long as she could stand it, Sarah went back indoors to see the secretary again. She warmed up and sat down to have a nice chat. By now there was only an hour left before Susan would be off work. Sarah borrowed the phone from the secretary and called Susan's workplace.

"Hi, Susan, this is Sarah. I'm back in town. I wondered if I could come over to see you this evening."

Susan almost shouted, "Oh, Sarah! I have missed you so much. Where are you?" Sarah told her that she was at her church and that she had just finished visiting her mom and dad.

Sarah said, "I can get a taxi to your place. What time are you planning to be home?"

Susan quickly thought about Paul and what she should do about him. She said, "No, Sarah. I can pick you up in my car. Don't get a taxi. I'm done with work in an hour. Will you wait there for me until I can come and get you in an hour and ten minutes?"

Sarah, who suddenly felt very tired, agreed. She told Susan to pick her up in the church office. She would stay with the secretary until she saw Susan.

Susan quickly called Paul at work to tell him the news. "Paul, it's Susan. I just got a phone call from Sarah. She's here, in town. She's at the church visiting her parents' graves. She agreed to let me pick her up in an hour."

Paul gave a shout of joy. "Susan, it's a miracle! I can't believe that she is finally back here where she belongs. Do you know anything about her situation yet?" he tentatively asked her.

Susan said, "No, I only talked to her for half a minute. All I know is that she is waiting for me to pick her up at the church."

Paul hesitantly asked her, "What do you think I should do?"

Susan did not want to tell him this, but she said softly, "Paul, you should let me go and get her and bring her back to my house. I don't have any idea what she will tell me or how she will be feeling. Will you just let me see her and make up my mind about her state of mind? I'm sorry, but I'm not sure that she is ready to see you. Can you wait for me to give you a call as soon as I know anything?"

Paul was very disappointed, but he knew that Susan was right. "Susan, please call me as soon as you can. Do me one favor, though. If Sarah is ill or anything like that, call me right away. Please, Susan," he begged her.

Susan knew what he was thinking. She agreed to call him the minute she could after deciding how Sarah was feeling. "Paul, you know I will. I will keep her safe with me. Don't worry, you will have the chance to see her. I promise." Susan gently reassured him.

Paul agreed and told her to call him on his cell number at any time. He would clear his schedule for the rest of the day and tomorrow in anticipation of seeing Sarah again.

Susan quickly walked into the church. She anxiously looked around, not wanting to miss Sarah. What if Sarah decided to disappear again before she could drive her home? She saw, with relief, Sarah coming out of the restroom. They ran towards each other and hugged fiercely. Susan felt how fragile Sarah was. Sarah's new slimness made her seem so small and frail. Susan took in Sarah's new haircut. Her hair was very shiny and swinging elegantly around her shoulders. It was the shortest haircut that Susan had ever seen on Sarah. As they hugged, Susan noticed that Sarah was wearing a ring on her left hand. She thought it looked like Sarah's mother's wedding ring. Susan decided not to mention it yet.

"Well, my friend, should we go home? Are you finished talking with your mom and dad?" asked Susan, with a grin.

"Oh yes, I have already taken my gift of flowers to their graves and talked as long as I could stand it, in the cold," said Sarah with a shiver. "Wow, I forgot how very cold it gets here in January."

Susan laughed and said, "You haven't been gone THAT long, my friend."

They picked up all of Sarah's luggage and packages from her earlier shopping expedition. When they were settled in Susan's car, she looked at Sarah and said, "Why don't you close your eyes for a bit until we get home? It always takes a little longer to get through this evening traffic. There will be enough time to talk once we are sitting, all cozy, in my living room." Susan looked at Sarah and told her firmly, "Of course, you will stay with me for as long as you want. Consider my home to be your home for the foreseeable future."

Sarah nodded, quite weary by now. She closed her eyes and sat back for the comfortable ride. Susan put the heat in the car on high and some soft music on low, and drove to her home, her precious cargo asleep beside her.

Once at Susan's house, she looked at Sarah and softly said, "You can't believe how glad I am that you are here. I have missed you so much! I've been so worried about you, Sarah. First things first, are you okay? Do you feel alright? I have been wondering if you were ill when you went away. And now, look at you, you've lost a lot of weight."

Sarah looked at her best friend and sighed. "Yes, I'm fine. I have been so unhappy over these past three months that it was hard to eat properly. I think that I have walked about a thousand miles, trying to outrun my thoughts and hopeless feelings."

Susan looked at Sarah and decided to tell her a little about Paul. "I want to hear all about where you have been and what you have been doing these past three months. But before that, I want to tell you something that I think will make you feel better." Sarah looked at Susan quizzically.

"Sarah, I ran into your Paul, accidentally, about a month ago. He was eating at the same restaurant that I was at. I was on a date. I saw this man staring at me. He came over and introduced himself. He said that he recognized me from the picture that you had in your apartment. You had told him that we were good friends. I sent my date home, and he and I talked for a few hours about you." Sarah just stared at Susan, saying nothing.

Susan went on, "He has looked for you everywhere. When he saw me, he hoped that I would have information about where you had gone. Sarah, he broke his engagement with Belinda the day that you left here."

Sarah couldn't believe it, "Paul broke his engagement? Then why did he hire Jim Bacon to take over my job?"

Susan said gently, "Why don't you talk to Paul about all of that? I know that he is dying to see you and talk with you again. Will you let me call him? He told me once that he would do anything in his power to see you again. I am sure that he would come over if you would agree to that. After you two have talked, maybe you could tell us both about where you have been and why you had to leave us." Susan looked hopefully at Sarah.

Sarah was tired, but she wanted above all things to see dear Paul's face again. She said quietly, "Yes, Susan, I want to see him. Will you call him?"

Susan beamed a huge smile at Sarah. "I'll call him right now. Maybe we can even have supper together after you have talked with him." Sarah nodded.

Susan ran to the phone and dialed a number. "Paul, Sarah is here, at my house right now. She wants to see you. I told her that you were not engaged to Belinda anymore." She listened for a few seconds, and said, "No, come over now. You can see her and talk, and then we can maybe have supper together." She laughed and hung up. She turned around and looked at Sarah. "He hopes that he won't get caught for speeding. He will be right here."

Sarah looked worried and a little withdrawn. "What if he doesn't love me? I don't think that I could bear it if I saw him, and he just wanted to be friends with me."

Susan started to tell Sarah something but changed her mind. It was Paul's right to tell Sarah how much he loved her. It was only right for him to be the one to tell her something that she longed to hear.

Susan said soothingly, "Sarah, he would hardly want to come tearing over here, risking a speeding ticket, to see you, if he did not care about you. You will know soon enough. He thought that he could be here in fifteen minutes. Why don't you relax, maybe wash your face and brush your hair before he gets here? I'm going into the kitchen to see what I have in the fridge for supper. Maybe we will feel like celebrating and want to go out to eat!"

Sarah went off into Susan's spare bathroom to tidy herself. She was pale but feeling very hopeful. She could not wait to see Paul and hear what he had to say. Susan went back into the living room to wait with Sarah. The doorbell sounded loudly in the quiet room. Both girls looked at the door, and then at each other. Susan said, "I'll get it. You just stay there and relax."

She opened the door with a flourish, and Paul rushed into the living room. He was holding a huge bouquet of red roses. His eyes sought out Sarah's eyes. His face was filled with a tender and loving expression. He took in Sarah's new hairdo and her extreme slenderness. She looked wonderful, not sick or unhealthy. He slowly walked to the couch where Sarah was sitting. He reached down and gently pulled her to her feet. She looked at him, too, saying nothing, just staring at his beloved face. His arms slowly went around her, afraid to scare her in any way.

Paul held Sarah with exquisite gentleness. He trembled as he looked down at her bent head. "Sarah, my beautiful sweet girl. These flowers are for you," he spoke, softly and gently. She took the roses and buried her face in their glorious scented stalks. Paul continued, "I have missed you so very much. I didn't know if you were alive or dead. Will you please talk with me and tell me why you ran away?" He kissed the top of her shiny hair. "But first, let me tell you how much I love you. You are the most delightful and enchanting woman that I have ever known. I don't think that I can go on without you in my life." Paul had a tremulous smile on his face as he stared down at her.

Sarah looked up at Paul, tears swimming in her soft green eyes. "Paul, I have dreamed of this day for three months. I never thought that you would be free from Belinda, or that you really loved me. I can't believe that this is happening to me."

Paul held her a little away from himself and looked at her carefully. "You have gotten so slim and cut your hair. I like the hair, it suits you. Are you feeling alright?" he asked anxiously.

She laughed a little and said, "I couldn't eat because I was missing you so much. I have walked miles and miles each day, trying to find a way that I could live my life without you in it."

Paul's heart gave a leap. He was overjoyed by what he just heard her say. "Oh, my dearest Sarah. We need to talk. But the only thing that I can think about is asking you to be my wife. Sarah, my sweet darling, will you marry me? And soon, because we have wasted so much time already." He looked anxiously at her dear face.

The sweetest smile was hovering on her lips. "Oh Paul, I love you, too. I couldn't bear it if I didn't marry you. And we can marry as soon as you like."

Paul laughed softly and said, "I'd like to marry you tonight! But I suppose that I could wait a week or two. Do you think that we could get married as soon as that? It is for you to decide, but I want to rush you down that aisle as soon as possible."

She smiled at him and said, "I don't want to wait, either. I think, with Susan's help, that I could marry you in two weeks." He kissed her then with a powerful gentleness that brought tears to her eyes. He brought her hands up to his mouth to kiss them. For the first time, he noticed her mother's wedding ring.

He looked at her and asked in a puzzled voice, "Why are you wearing a wedding ring?"

Sarah laughed a little shyly, "I pretended that I was engaged. I did not want my co-workers to ask me out. I just wanted to be left alone. I'll explain when I tell you my story. Oh, by the way, I told everyone that I was engaged to you, Paul."

Paul's eyes were very bright with happiness. "And so, you are-- engaged to me--I mean. Now, my love, let us sit down comfortably while you tell us where you have been and what you have been doing. We need to get Susan from the kitchen, first."

Susan had gone into the kitchen the minute Paul had arrived. She wanted to give them their privacy. She could hear a little of their conversation, so she knew that they had wonderful news. She grinned at Paul when he peeked his head around the kitchen door.

"Susan, you are a dear girl. Please come into the living room and hear what Sarah has to tell us about her whereabouts these past three months."

She sped past him and sat down on a comfy chair near the couch. Paul sat back down on the couch and pulled Sarah next to him. He put his arm around her shoulders and held on to her hand. Both Paul and Susan looked at Sarah with love and tenderness. They waited for her to speak.

It took a minute or two for her to gather her thoughts. Sarah started with the last day that she had seen Paul, the day he had kissed her in his office. She told him about the shock of meeting Jim Bacon, and finding out that Paul did not want her as his secretary anymore. Paul made a small sound of protest and would have interjected, but Sarah told him to wait until she finished her story. He would have his chance to tell his story after she had told them everything they wanted to know. Sarah told them about her job in Brazil and the new friends she had made there. She told them that they were holding her job for her in case she wanted to go back. At that piece of information, Paul pulled Sarah closer to him. Sarah smiled gently; it felt like Paul never ever wanted to let her go again. She looked at them both and continued her story. They all teared up when Sarah described just how lonely and sad she felt every evening. She admitted that she found the job interesting, but now that she had Paul's love, she definitely did not plan to go back there to work--although she would miss seeing her friends.

Paul listened carefully to everything she told them and then said that he would not mind if they stopped off in Brazil on their honeymoon and went to see her friends, just to say goodbye. Sarah thought that it was a generous offer and told him so. She was kissed very thoroughly for that. They just sat there, holding hands while she finished her story. Susan, wiping tears off her face, went back into the kitchen to make them all a cold drink.

Now it was Paul's turn to tell his story. He told her everything, from his plan to break up with Belinda, to his hiring of Jim Bacon.

"I am such a fool, darling," he told Sarah. "I knew that after I broke up with Belinda, I was going to ask you for a date. You see, I had already fallen deeply in love with you by then. You are such a very lovely person, and you are quite the most beautiful girl in the world." He continued, "I hoped that you had some feelings for me. You see, my sweet Sarah, you could show a cool and polite smile to me at work, but your beautiful eyes told me that you cared about me. I did not want to be dating you while you were working for me. I came back from Los Angeles full of plans for us. I was impatient, and it caused you to flee from me. Can you ever forgive me for the pain that I put you through?" he asked her humbly.

She looked at him with love and happiness. "Oh, Paul, I never even imagined that you hired Jim because you loved me and wanted to be with me so much. I was devastated when I thought that you wanted me to leave the job. I'm so happy that I was wrong. I am only sorry that I left without talking to you about it. I could have saved three months of heartache if I had had the courage to ask you about Jim."

She looked at Paul so sorrowfully that he hugged her gently. "No, my dear, it was all my fault. After I kissed you that Monday, and it felt like heaven, by the way, I should have asked you to talk with me when I got back from Los Angeles. I forgot to tell Jim to stay away until the day I wanted him to come to work for me. It would have given me a week or so to tell you that I was free and that I loved you. He could have taken over for you, and that would have left you free to date me. Hiring Jim, without first talking with you, was the biggest mistake I ever made in my life."

Sarah snuggled closer to Paul. She smiled at him. He looked at her, not quite yet believing that she was here and that she loved him, too. He couldn't wait to plan their wedding, and even more so, to begin their lives together. "Don't ever leave me, again, my love," he told her fiercely.

"I won't want to, Paul. You are my life. You are the only one I will ever love." Sarah whispered softly to him. Both Sarah and Paul, never having felt this kind of love for anyone before in their lives, found themselves unable to stop hugging and kissing each other. Finally, hand in hand, they walked into the kitchen to get Susan.

Paul told the two ladies that he wanted to take them out for a great steak. Susan put up a token resistance, saying that they should be alone to celebrate. Paul easily talked her into going with them. Sarah finished changing into a pretty dress before Susan did. She came out of the bedroom and stood there, just gazing at Paul. He caught her looking at him and grinned. His arms held her close to him, and he gave her a long and tender kiss. She lost her breath for a second and said, on a sigh, "Oh my, any more of those on my empty stomach, and I'll swoon."

He laughed delightedly and asked her, "Exactly what is a swoon? I've heard of it, but don't think that I have ever seen anyone actually swooning."

"Oh, I don't know--I thought it meant fainting from extreme pleasure," Sarah said with a smile.

Paul laughed softly and said, "Okay, go ahead. I promise to catch you when you swoon. It will be something to tell our children when they ask us about the night we became engaged."

"Never mind, Casanova, I think that I can make it through the evening without swooning," she said with a laugh.

Paul's eyes gleamed with happiness. "Oh, you never know. The night is not over yet, my love," he whispered softly into her ear. Sarah looked up at Paul, with stars in her eyes, and smiled with the sweetest smile that Paul had ever seen. Paul hugged her tightly and then stood there, with his arms around her while they waited for Susan to come out of her bedroom.

Susan walked out of her bedroom grinning. The bedroom walls were thin enough for her to have heard all about Sarah's swooning. She thought, with a pang, that Sarah would have Paul from now on. Their friendship might suffer a bit for a while after Sarah married Paul. How she wished that she could find a 'Paul' for herself.

They had a wonderful and light-hearted evening at the steakhouse. They all ate steak and drank champagne, talking and laughing. When Paul dropped them off at Susan's house, he stayed for only a few minutes. Susan hugged Paul and thanked him for the lovely dinner. She walked to her bedroom, saying good night over her shoulder. Paul pulled Sarah close to him, and they just hugged fiercely for a few minutes. He kissed her very thoroughly and then reluctantly let her go.

"Sleep well, my love. I don't think that I will ever forget this evening. It has been the happiest day of my life, so far. Having you back in my life has made me the happiest man in the world. I cannot wait until we are married, and we can wake up next to each other every day for the rest of our lives," Paul said softly to Sarah.

Sarah looked so lovely, with her shining eyes, flushed cheeks, and happy smile. "Paul, you have made me the happiest woman in the world. I just can't quite believe that we are together and that you love me, too. When will I see you tomorrow?" she asked him.

Paul told her that he would be there by 7:45 am with breakfast for all of them before Susan had to leave to go to work. He went home, set his alarm for 6:00 am, and joyfully went to bed. That night he had the best dream ever about Sarah. He dreamt that they got married amid a snowstorm, with all of his family looking on, smiling and covered with snow.

THIRTEEN

The next morning, Paul jumped out of bed when his alarm rang. He could not wait until he saw Sarah again that morning. He dressed quickly, called his office and left a few messages for Jim, and then took his dogs for a brisk walk in the snow. He drove to his favorite breakfast place, ordered a lavish breakfast for three people 'to go', got back into his car, and carefully drove to Susan's house. He arrived five minutes early and rang the doorbell. Sarah came to the door, rosy from her shower, looking good enough to eat. After a quick hard kiss on her lips, Paul went into the kitchen and carefully placed the food on the table.

Susan looked at the bags, and then at Paul, and said, "Oh you dear man, how did you know that Sarah and I love the food from this place? Wow, I could get used to having someone bring me breakfast every morning."

"Well, don't expect me to bring it every morning, my friend. I had to get up an hour earlier than usual to go there, order it, wait for it, then drive over here. But I promise that Sarah and I will bring you breakfast on your birthday and a few other special days, ok?" he said with a smile.

"Perfect," Susan grinned. "Thank you." Sarah was taking out all of the containers, curious as to what he had brought them. The scrambled eggs, bacon, blueberry waffles with syrup, and bowls of fresh fruit looked very tasty.

"Yum," Sarah said out loud. "Look at all of these goodies. Susan and I could not have chosen better ourselves. Very commendable, Paul," Sarah said, lovingly.

"Just for that, you get a kiss," laughed Paul. He proceeded to kiss Sarah to her complete satisfaction.

"Hey, cut that out, you two. I need to eat breakfast and get on the road in about fifteen minutes. Eat this delicious food with me. You can kiss all you want after I have left for work," Susan said, with a laugh. They all dug into the good food, not talking very much. Susan grabbed her lunch from the fridge and told them that she would be back about 4:15 that afternoon.

As she walked out the door, she said saucily, "Get some planning done today, you two. I expect to hear all about your wedding plans when I come home. If you have any questions for me, call me at noon, when I have my lunch break. I will eat in my office today so that you can find me easily if you need to talk with me. Whatever you haven't finished deciding, we can hammer out when I get home this afternoon. Now be good, you hear?" she stated, laughing when she went out the door.

After she left, Paul and Sarah just looked at each other for an eon of time, smiling, and hugging each other. Then they got some paper and pens and went into the living room to start their plans. They put on some soft music, turned on the electric fire in the fireplace, and sat down together on the couch. Paul drew Sarah's head down onto his shoulder and kissed her soft hair.

"Today is the second happiest day of my life, so far, my love," he whispered softly to her. Sarah looked up at Paul with a lovely smile and beautiful shining eyes. Her happiness was apparent in every cell in her body.

"Me, too," she said, just as softly to him.

"Before we start to plan the wedding, may I tell you about the two dreams that I have had recently?" Paul asked.

Sarah smiled, and said, "Yes, please, Paul."

He told her about his first dream, and how he felt that God had given him a message that he would see Sarah again. He smiled tenderly when he mentioned their two small sons and sweet little daughter.

Sarah teared up and said, "Oh, Paul, I had a dream when I was in Brazil. I also dreamt that we were married and had two sons and a daughter. Do you think that our dreams will come true?"

Paul hugged her tightly and declared, "My biggest dream has already come true. You came back and you love me. We are going to marry in a few weeks. I don't think that I could ever be happy again without you in my life. I thank God for you, my love." Paul said with a quiver in his voice.

He then told her about the dream he had last night about their wedding in a snowstorm and his family watching and smiling at them while they were covered in snow.

She softly smiled at him. "I wonder if we will get married on a snowy day," she said, with a laugh in her voice.

They tried to be sensible and plan their wedding, but every hour or so, they stopped to hug and kiss each other. They were both so happy that they almost burst. Besides their wedding plans, they talked about what they wanted out of life, their careers, their friends, family, and a host of other things. They found that they very much were in sync with their wishes and dreams. They stopped for lunch. Paul ran out and picked up some pasta for them. They worked their way through most of the wedding planning by 4:00 pm. They had called Susan at noon to ask her to be Sarah's Maid of Honor. Susan had gladly accepted. They told her that she would know more about their plans when she got home.

Susan got home at 4:30 pm, carrying a bottle of very fine champagne. "Ok, friends, let me get comfy first. Then you shall tell me everything about the wedding while we drink our champagne," Susan stated.

They waited for Susan to come back into the living room. In the meanwhile, Sarah went into the kitchen to get the wine glasses and the cheese and crackers that they decided to snack on while they told Susan about their wedding plans. Susan came into the living room, decked out in snuggly sweats, a fuzzy sweater, and her fun Toucan Sam bird slippers.

"Ok, I'm all comfy, now. One of you, start talking," she said, with a laugh. Paul poured out the champagne, and they toasted each other before Sarah started to talk. They nibbled on the cheese and crackers, so they would not feel tipsy from the champagne. They all had quite a lot to do that evening, so they needed to keep themselves sharp for that.

They planned to decorate the reception hall with a rich dark red color for the wedding because it was the dead of winter. Sarah also stated that that color would look lovely on Susan, with her dark hair and eyes. Sarah was, of course, going to wear her mom's white wedding dress and veil. She would carry a bridal bouquet of red roses, with ivy and white carnations. Paul promised that the church would be awash with as many flowers as they could comfortably fit in it. His best friend, Mark, would be his best man.

"Susan, you will like Mark, I think," Paul stated firmly. "All my lady friends think he is quite something," he said with a smirk.

"What does that mean?" asked Susan, curiously.

"Well, he is tall, dark, and handsome, so I've been told by my sister and mom. Personally, I just know that he is great fun. He has a wicked sense of humor. I've known him most of my life. We went to school together. Oh, the stories I could tell you!" he said with a huge grin.

Sarah just shook her head at him and said, "You can tell us your stories later, my dear. First, we need to tell Susan everything she wants to know about the wedding."

"Ok," said Susan, "But I definitely want to hear those other stories later, Paul." She was intrigued about her counterpart in the wedding. She had often heard of the Maid of Honor and the Best Man having a wonderful time together at a wedding. She currently did not have a boyfriend. It would be nice to have a fun little fling with a good-looking man at her best friend's wedding.

They had all had a very full day, so Paul left by 10:00 pm. He hugged Susan and thanked her for her hospitality. He hugged and kissed his dear sweet Sarah with a very happy heart. His eyes and his whole body seemed to be smiling whenever he looked at or thought about Sarah.

The next day he got somewhat caught up on his work in the morning and went to pick Sarah up at Susan's house at 12:30 pm. She was waiting nervously, but she looked lovely in a dark green velvet dress and high black fashion boots. He thought that she was the prettiest woman in the world. He just knew that his family would love her, too. He felt like the luckiest man on earth to be marrying her.

They went first to the church and talked with her priest. The priest was open to marrying them on the 25th of January, which was just sixteen days away. Because it was January, the reception hall was not booked for Friday, January 25th.

After they had seen the priest and the manager at the reception hall, Paul drove them back to his office. He had called Jim on his cell phone and asked him to get as many of his employees as possible to be there in the break room at 3:30 pm. Jim asked him what the meeting was about, but Paul just said that they would all know soon enough.

It was bittersweet for Sarah to return to her old office. They got out of the car, stopping while Paul took a few bottles of champagne and plastic wine glasses out of his trunk. He handled Sarah the bag of wine glasses, while he held onto the bottles of champagne. They walked into the office at precisely 3:30 pm. Only Jim was sitting at his desk. The rest of the employees were in the breakroom. Jim looked at Paul, and then at Sarah, and his jaw dropped. Then he began to smile widely.

"Come in, come in. Everyone is waiting for you in the break room." He led the way to the break room, walking much more easily than when Sarah had last seen him. His leg had healed very nicely in the time that Sarah had been away.

Paul ushered Sarah into the break room in front of him. He was wearing a huge smile, and his blue eyes were twinkling with happiness. Everyone stopped talking as soon as they got through the door. They looked at Sarah, and then at Paul, and their eyes opened widely. No one spoke, but they looked at the champagne in Paul's hands.

Paul smiled broadly, and said, "Everyone, I think you all remember Sarah Brewster. In sixteen days, she will become Sarah Thompson." Sarah smiled but couldn't speak because she had a huge lump in her throat. Everyone surged forward, hugging both Sarah and Paul, and shouting, "Congratulations!" Paul handed Jim the bottles of champagne, which Jim proceeded to open with the help of a few other employees who were near him. They poured the champagne into the plastic wine glasses that they took from Sarah's nerveless hands. When everyone had a glass of champagne, Jim called for a toast. The entire room raised their glasses in a rowdy toast to Paul and Sarah. Everyone laughed and talked for about ten minutes, finishing off all of the champagne. Paul told them that they were all invited to the wedding on the 25th of January. He would close the office that day so that everyone would have a chance to attend the wedding if they chose to.

A few people started to ask Sarah where she had been for three months. Paul interrupted them and told them that he and Sarah needed to leave for other appointments that evening. He told them that Sarah would come into the office the next day and catch everyone up on her news. With that, they had to be satisfied. Their curiosity was high, but they figured that they could wait a day to find out all about Sarah and Paul.

When Paul and Sarah got back into Paul's car, he turned to her and asked her quietly what she wanted to say to them.

"We haven't talked about what we want to tell anyone, darling. Do you want them to know our story? I'm sure that some of my employees have guessed, quite correctly, that I was pining away for you. I was a bear to everyone for nearly three months while you were away. It was only after that first dream about you that I even smiled at the office. I think Jim was on the verge of quitting because I was such a bad-tempered man to be around. Now they have seen you again, and I was smiling like an idiot. They can probably guess that you left because of me and that I was very unhappy about that. I will say anything you want me to say, my love. Please tell me what you are thinking." Paul said quietly.

Sarah had been thinking about that very thing all morning while Paul had been at work, and she now said, "Paul, I would like to tell everyone the truth, or at least a version of the truth. We will hopefully be colleagues and friends with these people for many years to come. I don't want to have to remember and then tell a lie for the rest of my life," she looked frankly at him.

"Whatever you want, my love. I agree that it would be simplest to tell them the truth, or at least most of it," Paul said gravely.

He held her hands and squeezed them gently. They talked in the car for a while, before deciding to go out for an early supper. While they were eating, Paul used his cell phone to call his mom, brother, and sister. His brother and sister agreed to meet at their mom's place at 7:30 pm. That gave Paul and Sarah a little while to eat and talk and get ready to tell Paul's family about their upcoming wedding. Paul explained that he had confessed everything to his brother after Joe had asked him straight out what was bugging him. Paul had moped around in a funk for months, and Joe said that the family just could not stand it anymore. They wanted to know what was going on with Paul.

Paul had told him that he had fallen deeply in love with the most beautiful girl in the world, his lovely secretary. They already knew about Sarah being his secretary because he had spoken of her often in the seven months they had worked together. They all thought that Belinda would be the wrong wife for Paul, and they were ever so happy when he told them that he and Belinda had broken off their engagement. He had told Joe that Sarah had abruptly left his employ while he was in Los Angeles. Paul had not known the reason for Sarah's departure, only that he was sick with worry about her and longing for her to come back into his life.

When Paul and Sarah went into his mother's house, hand in hand, he looked at his mom and forgot everything that he had planned to say to them. He pulled Sarah close to him and blurted out, "Mom, I want you to meet Sarah, the love of my life. She has agreed to marry me in sixteen days. I am the happiest man on earth."

His happy face and bright eyes told them that he was happier than he could even say. They loved Sarah on sight because she made their Paul look that way. They all came forward to hug first Paul, and then Sarah. Paul told Joe that he had some champagne in the trunk of his car and asked him to get it for him. He tossed Joe his car keys. Paul then brought everyone else into the living room and sat them down in the comfortable chairs. He sat on the couch with his arm tightly around Sarah's shoulders. They smiled at each other while they waited for Joe to come back with the champagne.

Everyone drank their champagne and waited for Paul to speak again. He introduced Sarah properly this time. Sarah shyly said hello to Paul's family. They were enchanted with her. She was a sweet and lovely young lady, and they could tell that she loved Paul just as much as he loved her. Paul waited until they had all finished drinking their glass of champagne, and then he began to tell them the whole story. He kept his eyes on Sarah's flushed face the entire time that he was talking. After he finished talking, there was not a dry eye in the house.

Paul's mother was crying quite openly. She leaned forward and clasped Sarah's hands. She thanked Sarah for loving her son. Sarah, with tears rolling down her cheeks, kissed her future mother-in-law on the cheek and thanked her for raising such a wonderful man. Paul told them about their wedding plans.

He had already asked Sarah if he could have Joe and Kelly as bridesmaid and groomsman in the wedding. Sarah had agreed, happily. When Paul asked them to be part of the wedding, they both agreed fervently.

Sarah told them that she did not have any family left and that an old family friend would walk her down the aisle. Paul's mother told Sarah that she was sad to hear about her lack of family, but that she now would have all of them, and they would be happy to be her family. Sarah was really touched by this. She had been nervous about meeting Paul's mother, but now she could see that they would have a wonderful relationship.

When they left his mother's house, Paul drove Sarah home. As they sat in the car in front of Susan's house, Paul held Sarah close in his arms for a long time, resting his cheek on top of her silky hair. He was full of contentment and love. He kissed her with tenderness and then knocked on Susan's door. Susan opened the door, saw how tired Sarah was, and ushered her to bed. Sarah slept deeply that night, happier than she had ever been.

After seeing Susan off to work the next morning, Sarah sat down and thought about what she would say to her old friends at Thompson Engineering. In the end, she decided to tell them exactly what had happened, only leaving out Paul's kiss and the scene in his office that Monday before he had left to go to Los Angeles. Her story would start with the unexpected arrival of Jim Bacon at the office that infamous Tuesday. Because both Susan and Paul were at work, Sarah used a taxi to get to the office.

Sarah peeked around Paul's office door when she arrived. He told her to come in and close the door. He called Jim on the intercom to tell him to hold his calls and any visitors for ten minutes while he talked with Sarah. Jim grinned at that and promised sincerely to keep everyone out for at least ten minutes. Sarah came into Paul's office and sat down in front of his desk. She had not been in there since the day she had left him her farewell note. They both sat for a few moments remembering that note. Sarah thought of the note with sadness, while Paul remembered his rage and hopelessness. Sarah came over to Paul and hugged him tightly.

"I'm so sorry, Paul, about that note I left you. I couldn't write anything else. My feelings were threatening to choke me at that moment," she apologized softly to him.

He crushed her to him and couldn't speak. The look in his eyes made her want to weep. He finally said, "It was the single worst moment in my life. I can't even put into words how awful I felt when I read your note. I wanted to die at that moment," Paul said tightly.

His eyes were dark and stormy. They just held each other for a few minutes. When Sarah gently broke away, Paul tried to smile. They knew that they had to move onward past that bad memory.

Sarah told Paul that she was ready to go into the break room and tell her old friends their story. She told him that she was not going to tell them about his first kiss. That memory was just for them. Their story would begin with the arrival of Jim Bacon on that Tuesday morning. Paul agreed and asked her if she wanted or needed him to be there when she told them.

Sarah said, "No Paul, I can do this by myself. I know that you have work to do. When I am done, do you want me to come back here to see you, or should I take a taxi back to Susan's house?"

"No, my love, don't take a taxi. I will take a few minutes off and drive you back there. In fact, let's have an early lunch while we are at it."

"Are you sure, Paul?" she asked.

"Yes, my dear. I want to see you safely back to Susan's house. Let me do that for you. I find that I want to know where you are and know that you are safe, all of the time," he said sheepishly.

Just for that, Sarah gave him a big hug and reached up to kiss his chin. She grinned and told him that she would see him when she was done in the break room.

She went into the break room. Several of her old co-workers were there. She sat herself down comfortably and told her story to as many people as were there. They were all so happy that she had come back home and had agreed to see Paul. They all wished her a happy life. Lots of hugs later, Sarah left the break room. She knocked on Paul's office door and waited for him to call out for her to come in. She told him about her talk with some of her old co-workers. Paul told her that he needed to finish something and would need about half an hour. Sarah went out into the waiting room and chatted with Jim Bacon. He told her about his quiet wedding to Betty. They talked about the job. Sarah found it interesting to hear Jim's opinions about his job. She missed working for Paul. They were still deep in a discussion when Paul came out of his office, coat in hand. He walked over to her, kissed her on top of her head, and asked her if she was ready to go. He took her out to eat at her favorite seafood restaurant. Since he had to plan for a lecture and several meetings, he dropped her off fairly early at Susan's house and told her that he would see her after work the next day.

CHAPTER

FOURTEEN

That first week went by so fast. Sarah remembered to call Mary Edwards. "Hi Mary, this is Sarah. How is everyone there?" she asked Mary in a cheerful voice.

"Oh Sarah, I was just thinking about you. How has your week at home been? You sound remarkably upbeat and happy," Mary said, with a smile in her voice.

"Mary, Paul and I are getting married on January 25th. I am just so happy that I could burst into song," Sarah said to her. "I know that you all probably can't make it to our wedding, but let me give you my friend Susan's phone number and address, just in case. Paul told me that we could stop off in Brazil to see you all on our way back from our honeymoon in Hawaii. I am still in shock-- this week has been the happiest one of my life," Sarah told her. They talked for a few more minutes and hung up, both smiling and happy. Mary told the others about Sarah's news.

Senor Santos was visiting them at the time and looked disappointed at Mary's news. He went about his business with a thoughtful look on his face. When he left the mine, he knew just what he wanted to do--see Sarah one more time. He had not been able to get her out of his mind. It was such a pity that he had, at last, found someone who he felt he could love, and she was taken. Well, she was not married yet, he thought. He decided to go and see Sarah and see if he could change her mind. He knew that he was a good catch. He could give her anything she desired. He was young and fit enough to make her happy with him, too, he thought. He got Susan's address from Mary. Since he told her that he wished to send Sarah a wedding present, Mary gave it to him without another thought.

Senor Santos pulled up to Susan's house in his rented Mercedes Benz around four in the afternoon on Friday, January 18th, one week before the wedding. On the passenger's seat was the huge bouquet of red roses that he had stopped to buy after his flight had come in. His dark good looks were enhanced by his elegant suit and silk shirt and tie. He picked up the roses and rang Susan's doorbell. Sarah was alone for the moment--Paul and Susan had not arrived yet from their jobs. Sarah was surprised when she looked through the peephole and saw Senor Santos standing there. She opened the door to him.

"Senor Santos, please come in," Sarah told him in a surprised voice.

"Ola, Amorzinho," he said softly to her. He handed over the roses. "I hear that you are to be married soon," he said in a sad voice. "Oh, Sarah, eu gosto muito de você," Senor Santos said softly. "I have come to see if you are really sure that you want to marry this Paul person. I have not been able to forget you, my dear Sarah. I would be very good to you. You could have everything that you ever wanted, if you just let me love you," he said passionately to her.

Sarah was so surprised that she could not say anything at first. "Senor Santos, I'm sorry that you came all the way here to see me, but I love Paul, and I am going to marry him next week. He is everything that I have ever wanted," Sarah said, just as passionately as he had been a moment before.

"Thank you for the flowers, but I really think that you should go now," she said firmly to him.

He looked at her for a minute, then nodded sadly. "If you ever decide that you and Paul are not right for each other, please give me a call. I would be here on the next plane." He put his business card with his private number on it on the counter with the roses. He kissed Sarah's cheek and let himself out the door.

Paul, who had arrived a minute before, parked behind the Mercedes. Through the window, he saw Senor Santos kiss Sarah's cheek. He felt an unwelcome rage sweep over him at the sight of Senor Santos' kiss. Paul did not like this very jealous side of himself. There had to be a reason for what he was seeing. He was just about to knock on the door when Senor Santos came out of the house.

He looked Paul up and down and said strongly in his passionate voice, "Are you Sarah's Paul? I just want to tell you that you had better treat her like the queen that she is. If you hurt her, I will know, and I will not stand by to see it happen." With that, he got into the Mercedes.

Paul had to get back into his car and move it so that Senor Santos could leave. Paul was furious. He strode into the kitchen and saw the red roses. Sarah was just standing there, looking numb. Paul came closer and saw Senor Santos' business card with his personal telephone number on it, sitting there right out in the open. He felt so hurt. "Who was that man, and why did he act so possessive about Sarah?" he wondered. Why had he given Sarah red roses, too? He wanted to talk with Sarah about it, but he was just so steamed that he felt he should cool off before talking with her.

"I forgot something at the office. I have to go," Paul told Sarah very abruptly.

He turned around and strode out the door. Sarah just looked after him, shocked. She wanted to talk with Paul and explain about Senor Santos. She had done nothing wrong. She knew that it looked bad, but she was not responsible for Senor Santos' actions. She had never allowed him to think that she was available. It was just that he was a handsome millionaire who apparently felt that he could have anything he wanted--and he had wanted Sarah.

Because she loved all flowers, she could not bring herself to throw the roses away. Still in shock, she found a vase and stuck the roses in it. She put the roses in her bedroom so she would not have to talk to Susan about them. She sat down to think about what to do. Tears fell down her cheeks when she thought about Paul's reaction to seeing Senor Santos and the flowers. She would give him time to calm down, she decided. Then they would talk about it and laugh together, she hoped.

Susan came home just then. She saw Sarah's tears and asked her what was wrong. Sarah told her all about Senor Santos' surprising visit. She also told her who Senor Santos was and about her one date with him in Brazil.

Susan kindly told Sarah, "You don't have anything to apologize for, Sarah. You were on a harmless date with your boss. You told him that you were engaged before you went out with him. You said that he was a perfect gentleman on the date. It is not your fault if he has feelings for you. You tried to warn him off. Besides, you had not even talked with Paul when you went out with Senor Santos. Paul has no reason to be upset with you."

"Do you think I should call him, Susan?" Sarah asked anxiously.

"He's a big boy. Let him have a night to cool down. He will probably be here tomorrow morning, early, begging for your forgiveness for his stupidity, tonight," Susan said firmly and with conviction.

"Do you think so?" Sarah looked at Susan with big sad eyes.

"I'm positive about it," said Susan with a small grin. "Let's forget about it for a bit. I'm hungry. Let's have supper," Susan said positively.

The two friends tried to forget about it while they made and ate supper. After they had washed up, they went over the list of things that still needed to be done before the wedding. Sarah dragged herself off to bed, wondering what Paul was doing just then. She felt scared and unhappy for the first time since she had come back to Litton. They loved each other, she thought, tearfully. Why should something go wrong now, within sight of their wedding day?

Paul drove home like a demon was on his tail. He was mad at himself, but mostly he was hurt and jealous. Maybe Sarah had gotten to know and like that guy in Brazil. Why had she never mentioned him to Paul? He thought that he would wait another day until he felt really calm before he would go to Sarah and ask her about that fellow. He took the dogs for a very long walk before going to bed without his supper. He wasn't hungry for Mrs. Kennedy's good wholesome food. He had a bad dream that night. He couldn't really remember it in the morning, but it left him feeling wrung out and out of sorts. Paul went into the office for a bit and took care of a few things. Because it was Saturday, no one else was there. He ended up sitting at his desk for a long time, just thinking about Sarah. That was why he was not at his home in the early afternoon when Sarah tried to call him. She called several times, each time getting his answering machine. By now she was really frightened and getting angry, herself. Where was Paul, and why didn't he call her or come to see her, she wondered with a heart that hurt her.

Sarah was not giving up on Paul, but she had decided to be a little cool with him when, or if, he ever called her. When she did not hear from him by two o'clock that afternoon, she asked Susan to borrow her car and took herself off to the mall to get a few things for the wedding. Since she was out, she stopped in to see Clara and Rip. She talked with Clara about the wedding, hiding the hurt she felt about Paul's silence. Clara could tell that Sarah was worried about something, but she didn't push her for information. Clara knew that Sarah would tell her if she felt she needed advice or just to get something off her chest.

Sarah left Clara's house feeling a little happier. She then made her way to Ben and Josie's house. They talked about the wedding, as well. Ben was so pleased to be walking Sarah down the aisle. Josie promised that she would do whatever Sarah needed to have done on the morning of the wedding. She was proud to be Sarah's personal attendant for the wedding.

Sarah finally turned for home, but it was now after 7:00 pm. She did not know that Paul had stopped by Susan's house at 4:00 pm when he had left his office. Susan had royally told him off for being a jerk. He went home and tried to eat the meal that Mrs. Kennedy had left for him. It all tasted like dirt in his mouth. He called Sarah on her cell phone, but she did not answer; she had accidentally left it in her car with her other purchases from the mall. He called Susan's house, and Susan coolly told him that Sarah had not come home yet. They could not have known that they kept missing each other. Both Sarah and Paul went to bed that night very unhappy and worried. It was now less than a week before the wedding, and they were not even speaking to each other. The longer they went without talking to each other, the more unhappy they felt.

Sarah awoke the next morning, determined to see and talk with Paul that day. She was just getting ready for church when the doorbell rang. She ran to the door, hoping with all her heart that it would be Paul. It was. They fell into each other's arms and just held each other, not speaking. Susan, who had come out of her bedroom to see who was at the door, went back into her bedroom, grinning like an idiot. Good, they made up, she thought, happily. She stayed in her room for another half hour, just to give them time together.

"Oh, Paul, thank you for coming. I was coming to see you after church today. I'm sorry if I did something to hurt you," Sarah said sadly.

Paul just hugged her tighter and said, "No, love. I'm the one who should be apologizing. You didn't do anything wrong. I was jealous of that guy who came to see you. I saw him kiss you. I should never have let him get to me. Will you please forgive me, darling?" he asked her humbly.

"Of course, dear Paul," Sarah said, in a happy voice. "Let me explain who Senor Santos is and why he came. Then you'll understand everything," she told him with urgency. Sarah told Paul everything about her interactions with Senor Santos. She explained that he had surprised her with his visit. While she had known that he was attracted to her, she had been unaware that he had such deep feelings about her.

"I can't really blame him," stated Paul, in a rueful voice. "You are such a beautiful, enchanting woman," Paul declared. "If I feel that way about you, I guess another man could feel that way about you, too. But I am over the moon that you chose me, my darling," Paul said reverently to Sarah. He kissed her fiercely and passionately. It was a long time before either of them had their breath back.

"I should tell Susan that she was right, I was a jerk," Paul said wryly. Susan had already come out of her bedroom and had gone into the kitchen while they had been kissing. Neither of them had even seen her pass them by.

Paul found Susan and said, "Susan, you were right. I was a jerk. Thank God that Sarah can forgive me. Will you forgive me, too, dear friend?" he asked her hopefully.

Susan just grinned and said, "Ok, cowboy, just don't be that stupid, again. Now let's get ready and go to church. I know that Sarah is going to want to talk with her mom and dad after the service. It's about time that you were introduced to them. After all, you will be their son-in-law--even if you can't see them," she added with a small smile.

The three friends went first to church, listening to the insightful words that the priest had to say. When the service was done, Sarah introduced Paul to some of her friends as they walked out of church. In the cemetery, Sarah laid down the flowers she had brought with her on her mom and dad's graves. She introduced Paul to them. She reminded them that Susan was paying her respects, as well. The three friends talked with great happiness about the wedding, which was now just five days away. Sarah promised to stop by and see them again before she got married.

Thursday evening, the night before their wedding, Paul and Sarah stopped off at the St. Mary's Shelter. It was 6:00 pm, and the parking lot lights were on, lighting up the basketball court. Paul had his big shovel with him. He was dressed for playing basketball in the snow. Sarah was dressed warmly, as well. Paul cleared a space for Sarah on the sidelines and then went back to his car to get the lightweight camping chair that Sarah would sit on. She got comfortable on the chair. Paul came back over to her, tucked a warm fuzzy blanket over her legs, and kissed the top of her head. Sarah looked around her. There was a great turnout for the game tonight.

She waved to Billy and Johnny when she saw them shoveling near the edge of the court. Sarah had gone to the game with Paul last Thursday and had met the boys, their mother, and Snuffles. Paul had properly introduced Johnny, Billy, and their mother, Judy, to Sarah. Way back in April, the boys had talked their mother into letting them play basketball at the shelter every Thursday evening. Judy had been so glad that they had a place to go and make friends that she had agreed to go as well and cheer them on. She always sat with Snuffles, watching her two sons play basketball and making some new friends. Judy was very grateful to Paul for the unobtrusive help that he had given her, too. He had introduced himself to her that first night, back in April. He had quietly asked her if she needed anything--money, clothes, food, anything. She had told him that she was almost able to make her rent payments but came up short by about fifty dollars every month. He had told her that he had met the boys at a grocery store and had invited them to play with the other kids on Thursday nights. He did not tell her about the incident with the dog and the groceries. Judy thought that he was very nice to keep that from her. She already knew all about it because Johnny and Billy had come clean and had told her all about it when they had asked to attend the basketball games. Judy had forgiven them. They were boys--her boys--and she understood that some things could get frustrating at times.

Paul had quietly given her the fifty dollars that she had needed for her rent, with the promise of fifty more dollars the next month, provided that the boys continued to come and play basketball each week. She had tearfully taken the money and thanked Paul profusely. Judy came to the games every week after that. In June, Paul had found Judy a part-time job, and that money was enough for her to pay all of her bills, and even sock a little away for a rainy day. She was very grateful to Paul and all that he had done to help her and her boys.

Last week, Paul had introduced her to Sarah. Her boys told her in a whisper that Sarah was the woman who had yelled at them for hitting Snuffles. Judy thanked Sarah for teaching her boys that they should never hit animals. Sarah and Judy had quite a long conversation while the basketball game was going on. They only stopped talking to cheer on their guys. Sarah was so very proud of Paul and the way he related to the kids who were there. He knew all of their names, as well as the names of their family members and pets that came to watch. The kids and their families all treated Paul with deference. They obeyed him, respected him, but most of all, really liked him.

After tonight's quick game, he took Sarah home so she could get ready for the groomsmen's dinner. Because of the basketball game, no one was planning to be there until 8:30 pm. He went home, took a shower, dressed up in his best suit, and drove back to pick up her and Susan.

Everyone in the wedding party, Paul's mother, and Ben and Josie were invited. The only one who was not there was his Best Man. Mark was flying in from New York, but he wouldn't arrive until quite late that night. The dinner party guests were light-hearted and full of fun. It was a fantastic evening. Paul took Susan and Sarah home by 11:30 pm. He told them to sleep well. He pulled his lovely Sarah into his arms for a long hug and tender kiss and then pushed her towards her bedroom and watched her go in and close her door. Then he turned to Susan.

"Watch over her tonight, Susan," he begged her softly. "Make sure that my love gets some sleep tonight. This is your last night to be her guardian angel. As of tomorrow, that will be my job. Then she will be under my care, forevermore."

Susan nodded, a huge lump in her throat. "Good night, Paul. Drive safely. See you in the morning," she said softly. Paul hugged Susan tightly. She had been a good friend to him while he was waiting for Sarah to come back to them. He gently kissed Susan's cheek and touched her shoulder in complete friendship and support. She opened the door for him. Paul turned and left, his heart full.

On the other side of her closed door, Susan leaned back against it and sighed, thinking to herself, "The journey that we have been on to find our lost friend is at an end, and I could not be happier for Sarah. Paul is a dear man. I only hope that I will find someone like him someday."

In her bed, Sarah was talking to her mom in prayer. "Tomorrow I will marry the man that I love with all of my heart, Mom. You always said that we would find each other. I hope that Paul and I will be as happy as you and Daddy are. Last October, I thought that I would never be happy again, but you knew differently, didn't you, Mom? There is someone for Susan, too, isn't there? I can't stand to think that she might be alone. I know that I will probably get caught up loving Paul and, later, our children. I don't want Susan to feel left out. I'll certainly try not to shut her out. How I wish that you and Daddy were here with me for the most special day in my life. I love you, Mom. Good night."

Paul drove himself to his bachelor home for just one more night. His heart was so full of happiness. He looked around his home, loving it. Soon it would shelter his wife and his babies. He put all of his clothes and other necessary things for tomorrow ready to go. He looked at the massive amounts of flowers that were in his living room. Mrs. Kennedy would arrange them in the morning in the lovely vases that he had bought. She would put some vases in every room, saving the most beautiful ones for their bedroom. He knew that he had been extravagant, but he didn't care. He wanted Sarah to come into their home tomorrow night and be overwhelmed by their gorgeous scent and beauty. She already knew about the masses of flowers at the church, but she had no idea that there would be more of them to greet her when he carried her over the threshold of their home.

He grinned when he thought of her probable reaction. She would probably shed a few tears, but underneath, she would be thrilled to bits. Mrs. Kennedy knew that she would be taking most of them to the church the next morning after they had left for their honeymoon to Hawaii. He left Mrs. Kennedy a note, reminding her that his cousin would pick her up at 9:30 am to drive her to the church for the wedding. "Mark should be arriving soon," thought Paul. He was supposed to pick up his rental car after his flight came in. Paul hoped that Mark would not be too late. Paul wanted a decent night's sleep. After all, tomorrow was the biggest day of his life. Sarah would finally become his wife. He thought back to last October and remembered that he didn't think he would ever be happy again. "Life was amazing sometimes," he thought with a big smile.

Mark arrived half an hour later. He gave Paul a big hug. They had been best friends since elementary school. They talked for another half hour before Mark shooed him into his bedroom and told him to get some shuteye. Mark promised that he would be up by 7:30 am to take the dogs for a walk while Paul leisurely ate breakfast and got ready for his wedding. Paul went to bed, tired, but extremely content.

FIFTEEN

January 25th dawned, cold and overcast. Sarah shivered when she left her warm bed. Susan had insisted that Sarah have breakfast in bed. She laughingly said that she expected to get breakfast in bed on her wedding day, and either her mother or Sarah would have to provide it. They sat on Sarah's bed and talked while she ate her breakfast. The wedding mass was scheduled for 10:00 am that morning. It was now 7:30 am. They had plenty of time to dress and get to the church to make sure that everything was right on schedule. Susan dressed first because she had promised to help Sarah into her wedding dress and veil. She looked lovely. The rich red velvet dress was a perfect foil to her wavy dark hair and big brown eyes. Susan was satisfied with her appearance. She knew that the dress was very beautiful and that she looked attractive in it. She went into Sarah's bedroom and helped her into her mother's wedding dress. They had had it cleaned, and now it looked so sweet and old-fashioned on Sarah. Sarah made a lovely bride, a little pale, but her eyes were shining. She looked like a tender young bride from the 1930's. They held off on putting on her veil. They could do that at the church. Susan went out to warm up her car. Huge snowflakes were starting to come down.

"Oh no, it looks like we might get that snowstorm that Paul had dreamt about," she said to Sarah when she went back indoors. Sarah just shook her head. She did not want anything to spoil this day--the biggest day of her life. Sarah could not believe that today she would finally marry Paul. She smiled softly and daydreamed a little until Susan reminded her that they should leave soon for the church. Susan drove carefully to the church because the roads were already starting to get slippery. There were already a dozen or so people there getting the church ready for the wedding. Paul's sister and mother were already there, as well. Susan greeted them cheerfully, while Sarah gave them a big hug.

"Paul's not here yet, is he?" Sarah asked them anxiously. She was a little superstitious about the groom not seeing the bride until the wedding.

Kelly grinned and said, "No, Joe and Mark are keeping Paul under wraps until 9:59 am. Don't worry, he won't see you until you start to walk down the aisle with your friend, Ben."

Sarah nodded and sighed in relief. She looked around her. The church was filled with incredible vases and pots of every kind of flower that Paul could buy. He had promised her that the church would be filled with flowers, and he had kept that promise. He must have bought out half of the flowers in the whole town. She was so touched by his lovely gesture. Her bridal bouquet was sitting in the front pew, where Paul's mother would be sitting. They had decided to put some red roses in a beautiful vase on a small table in the front of the church, next to the wedding picture of Daniel and Tilly Brewster. On the same table was a picture of Paul's father and a lovely bouquet of flowers for him. Sarah looked at the roses now; her eyes filled with tears at the thought of her mom and dad. How they would have loved to have seen this beautiful sight in their church. Sarah had visited their graves yesterday and had told them all about the wedding. She would visit the graves again in two weeks and tell them all about Hawaii.

Susan helped Sarah put on her veil. Sarah looked exactly like a young Tilly Brewster. Susan caught her breath, just looking at Sarah. They walked around the church, looking at everything. The ends of the pews were now draped with red velvet and lace bows. The wedding aisle was covered in a pretty white lace runner. The whole church looked so lovely and smelled divine.

Susan had not yet met Mark, the Best Man, because he had not arrived in time for the groomsmen's dinner the night before. Susan and Kelly had liked each other since the first time they met when Paul had invited them all to meet over a nice meal. They had seen each other a few more times in the last few weeks. She had liked Paul's mom and his brother, as well. Sarah was a lucky woman. She would have Paul's love and some very nice in-laws. Women were always a bit nervous about their mother-in-law, but Vivian Thompson was a sweetheart. Susan hoped that she would be as lucky when it came time for her to get married.

At 9:45 am, Susan and Kelly whisked Sarah into a small room where she could wait until it was time to line up in the church foyer. During this time, Mark and Joe would get Paul up to the altar to wait for Sarah to walk down the aisle. Sarah sat nervously, clutching her bouquet. She was pale, but she had such a look of love and anticipation on her face that Susan just had to give her a hug and kiss.

"You look so lovely, Sarah. Just sit quietly and take some deep breaths. Not long to go, now, love," Susan said quietly to Sarah. While they were waiting, they heard dogs barking and a bit of scuffling.

Kelly's face flushed, and she shook her head. "Oh, no, they didn't really do it, did they?" she whispered to herself.

She looked quickly at Sarah and told her that nothing was wrong. Mark had a surprise for them all. She wouldn't say anything else, though. The magic time had come. The girls went into the foyer, where they saw Ben. He was trying not to laugh. Sarah frowned at him, and he kissed her and said that he was ready. Susan twitched Sarah's veil into a precise waterfall just as the music started. The door opened, and Susan caught her first glimpse of her counterpart, Mark. She was stunned. He was the most gorgeous man that she had ever seen. He was grinning wickedly while holding onto the leads of Mutt and Jeff, Paul's two Labradors. They were wearing rich red velvet bow ties around their necks. He handed their leads to another young man as he stepped forward to take Susan's arm. The procession had begun. Mark and Susan went first, followed by Kelly and Joe. Sarah and Ben were next. Last of all was the young man leading Paul's two dogs down the aisle after Sarah. Sarah felt a hysterical giggle start to form, which she had to severely stifle. The dogs were surprisingly well-behaved as they walked down the aisle. Sarah looked at Paul, who was looking at her with such a loving and tender look on his face. He looked past her to see Mutt and Jeff walking towards him. He grinned for a quick second. That Mark, he thought, with an inward grin. It figures. He should have known that Mark would pull something outrageous today.

The wedding was lovely. All of the music was sung beautifully by the congregation. The sermon was heartfelt, and Paul and Sarah listened to every word of it. Their vows were poignant and brought tears to most of their guests' eyes.

As they walked arm in arm down the aisle after the wedding, Paul and Sarah looked around at all of the people they loved most in the world. This was a day for joy. Sarah's motto of always "Choosing Joy" could not have been more appropriate. Sarah looked so beautiful and happy. Paul felt like his heart was so full that it would burst. He was married to Sarah. She was now, and forever,

Mrs. Sarah Thompson. Sarah was feeling the same way that Paul felt. This was the happiest moment of her life.

A snowstorm was raging outside as the wedding party left the church in the limousine that Paul had hired. He had invited his mother to ride with the wedding party. Paul told Mark firmly that the dogs would not be going into the limo with them. Mark had grinned and agreed, his face showing none of the mischief for which he was well known. Photographers had taken some lovely pictures at the church. They were going to follow the limo to the reception hall, where they would take more pictures. The limo led the way to the reception hall and dropped them off right outside the big front door. Paul tenderly helped his new bride out of the car and into the building. The first thing he saw when he got into the reception hall was an enlarged life-size picture of himself from his college days. He was wearing a ripped-out shirt and straggly cargo shorts. Sarah stared at it. She burst out laughing and turned to look at Paul, questioningly.

"Mark, wait until I get a hold of you. Remember that I will get to pay you back for this when you get married someday," Paul said with a laugh.

Mark came over and took Sarah's hand. He gave her a big smacking kiss on her cheek and said, "Sarah, you are even more lovely than Paul said you were. I wish that I would have seen you first. Still, now that you are married to this guy, I hope that we will be friends. Paul has been my best friend for most of my life. I would do anything for him."

"It looks like you have already done that, Mark," Sarah said, cheekily.

"Oh Paul, you married a good one, here. I think she will suit you just fine," Mark said with satisfaction.

Mark turned around and asked the crowd, "Now where is that lovely Maid of Honor? I still need to introduce myself to her."

Susan came around the back of Sarah and grinned. "Hi, Mark, I'm Susan. Sarah is my best friend. We have been best friends since we were nine years old," she told him.

"What is that, about ten years then?" he asked her, with a saucy grin.

"Oh, how very gallant of you. Thank you, kind sir," said Susan sassily. They grinned at each other. "Today was going to be a fun day," thought Mark. "Today was going to be a fun day," thought Susan.

Paul had to put up with lots of laughter at Mark's "gift" to him. There were half a dozen enlarged pictures of Paul all over the reception hall, from the time he was eight years old to the present day. They all seemed to be pictures of Paul looking his worst, wearing his oldest and scruffiest clothes. Sarah whispered to Paul that, personally, she liked them and hoped that they would keep them at their home. They would be company for her in case he ever had to be away from home for a day or two. Paul just hugged her and laughed about that. The dogs stayed at the reception for an hour or two until Paul asked Mark to take them home. Mark good-naturedly agreed to get someone to take them home. One of Paul's cousins, who had walked the dogs down the aisle, would take them home. He was ready to leave, anyway.

Paul and Sarah had a lovely time at the reception. Champagne flowed generously and everyone felt very uplifted and light-hearted. At the wedding supper, Paul and Sarah kept everyone laughing when people clinked on the glasses to convey that the bride and groom must kiss. Paul good-naturedly and dramatically kissed Sarah every way he could think of--a big swoony kiss, a kiss on her nose, on top of her head, her hands, her cheeks, her neck, and back to her lips again. Sarah giggled and went along with everything Paul did, being an extremely good sport about it all. She actually loved the big swoony kisses the best and couldn't wait until they had some time to themselves to practice some more.

After a while, Paul told Mark that he would have to do his duty as the Best Man and take over some of the kissing. So, for his first kiss, Mark sweetly kissed Sarah on her nose. The next time he rushed over and gave Susan a big swoony kiss. They both looked quite shaken when they came up for air. Then Mark went down the line and kissed Kelly's cheek and then Vivian's hand. Amidst all of the laughter, he continued to sneak looks at Susan. Susan's cheeks were as bright a red as her lovely gown. Paul and Sarah led the dancing with a romantic waltz. After that first dance, others joined them on the dance floor. Mark danced once with Sarah. He dramatically swept her around the room in a beautiful dance. Mark was a sensational dancer--very light on his feet for being such a tall and lean man. He went on to dance with almost every woman at the reception. He danced the most often with his counterpart, Susan.

Sarah loved all of the dancing. She could have danced in Paul's arms all night, but she dutifully danced with all of their guests when she was asked to do so. Ben came over and quietly asked her to dance a slow waltz with him. He held her tenderly. He had thought of Sarah like a daughter for many years. Now, after walking her down the aisle that morning, he really felt like her father. He hugged her fiercely and begged her to be happy. Sarah reached up and kissed his sweet cuddly face with love. Her heart was full of love and friendship for Ben and Josie for all of the love and care that they had shown Tilly and herself for more than fifteen years.

Clara had come to the reception with Ben and Josie. "If I had known that dogs were invited to the wedding, I would have brought Rip," Clara laughingly told Sarah. Sarah and Paul laughed and told her that it was all Mark's deal. They had not expected to see Mutt and Jeff at the actual wedding.

"However, they behaved well, didn't they?" asked Paul, with pride for his dogs.

Clara, Josie, and Ben each gave Sarah a huge hug and kiss and said they had to leave. The wind was blowing, and the heavy snow kept falling. Soon most of the guests decided to make their way home through the snowstorm. Sarah saw Susan and Mark still dancing. They seemed to really like each other. Mark was holding Susan quite tightly. Every once in a while, he would dip her quite low to the floor. She would laugh and protest, but Sarah could tell that Susan was having a wonderful time. They were flirting outrageously with each other. Sarah looked at her new husband and smiled.

"One more dance, darling?" she asked Paul. He smiled and hugged her tightly. They danced their last waltz before going around and saying goodbye to everyone who was still there. Kelly and her husband would make sure that Vivian got home safely at the end of the evening. They would stay until the end and make sure that all of the food and presents got loaded into the van to go to Joe's house. Joe, his wife, and two boys would make sure that everyone else got away safely. Paul and Sarah would visit his house to open their wedding presents after they returned from their honeymoon.

Paul said something to one of his cousins, who brought the limo up close to the door. Paul helped Sarah into the limo, waving goodbye to whoever came out to see them off.

Once inside the limo, Paul leaned forward to tell his cousin, "Home, James." The driver grinned and said, "Right you are. Just sit back and enjoy the trip." Paul put his arms around Sarah and kissed her with a long and passionate kiss. "We'll soon be home, my lovely Mrs. Thompson," he said gently to Sarah. "Our home," he explained.

She reached up and kissed Paul with a sweet kiss. "Yes, my love, our home," she said with a happy sigh.